Pete Trewin was born in Middlesbrough under the shadow of the steel mills but has lived for most of his life in a leafy suburb of Liverpool with his wife, Paula and golden retriever, Eira. Their three children have long moved on.

While working as an economic development and regeneration consultant, Pete gained a knowledge of how you might launder ill-gotten money. Not direct experience, obviously. This set him on the path of writing crime novels. The rest of his time is spent in Snowdonia where he indulges his interest in rock climbing and hill walking.

Other books by Pete Trewin:

A Fair Wack
Time Lapse
Not Without Risk

Pool of Life

PETE TREWIN

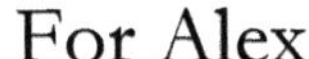

For Alex

'Liverpool is the pool of life...'
Memories, Dreams and Reflections Carl Jung

'Dead, Mr Pegotty?' I hinted after a respectful pause. 'Drowndead,' said Mr Pegotty.
David Copperfield Charles Dickens

'Water, water, water everywhere...'
The Water Song The Incredible String Band

CHAPTER ONE

Blast from the Past Hour on Radio City. So what do they start with? *Ferry Cross the Mersey.* Gerry and The Pacemakers. As far as Jack Gordon was concerned, a lot of those bands from the sixties—Freddie and the Dreamers and Herman's Hermits and the rest of them—should have been consigned to the dustbin of history where they belonged, not constantly resurrected. To the poets and philosophers, Liverpool was the pool of life. To Jack Gordon at this moment, it was a pool of shite.

He turned off the radio, put his road CD on for a bit, yawned and leaned back in the car seat. Everything But The Girl; *I need you, like the desert needs the rain.* Tracy Thorn's sultry voice. Now that was good music. From the 80s when he was a teenager.

Forty-eighth day without rain. The streets had been eerily quiet, people hiding from the sun. His underpants were sticky and twisted around his tackle. He squirmed until he freed himself, cursing at his stupidity. He'd bought the wrong ones in M&S— slips, thongs really—rather than the substantial boxers or trunks he preferred. Someone must have put them on the wrong rack.

Needing air, he turned off the CD and edged the car window down. Festival Park by the river. On surveillance. Prime dogging spot. A wood pigeon cooed at its partner in a nearby tree. Barry White and his sexy little lady friend, know what I'm saying? Pool of shite? No, that was unfair to Liverpool. It was the insomnia talking. Now that the dream had returned, he couldn't sleep and was grumpy all the time as a result. It must have been triggered by reading about that incident in the *Echo*.

The red and white tapes had still been there when he'd driven past. He'd stopped for a moment to take in the view of the river; yellow brown water heaved and surged where the strong, freshwater flow met an irresistible incoming tide in a display of incredible power, as if it were the Amazon or the Congo in flood. If you went in, you'd had it. Powerful enough to take the life of another innocent, this time a thirty-year-old woman who'd been jilted in love. It had been on the radio news that morning.

He hated how he always wore his heart on his sleeve like this. In his line of work, you were supposed to be the tough guy. It wasn't as if this kind of stuff didn't happen all the time in a city with a waterfront like Liverpool. The going gets tough? No, you don't get going, you jump in the water. Like that other girl all those years ago.

Splattered insects, bird droppings and a fine red dust—probably from the fires on the moors or carried over from the Sahara—covered the windscreen. Someone had written *SS Snoopers* in the dust on the car's rear window, but that was unfair. Jack's firm didn't get involved in that line of work. It was no use trying to take photos through the dirty car windows, so he lowered the one on the driver's side and poked the telephoto lens of the camera out. It was no use. He couldn't get the right angle. The big silver Merc at the other end of the car park bounced up and down on its springs, the occupants having a great time, but he couldn't get any shots of what was going on from where he was. He'd have to leave his car and creep up on them. Safe n' Secure usually used a special van for surveillance, where you could sit in air-conditioned comfort in the back and watch through one-way windows, but it was in the garage for repairs.

Take the car to the garage? Chance would be a fine thing. The air con on this car wasn't working properly, and he didn't have the time to get it fixed. So he'd had to drive with the windows open and suffer the foul air rammed with impurities, pollen and traffic fumes.

Lucy had informed him as he arrived at the office that morning that his two key operatives hadn't turned in. So he had to take up the urgent work himself. The CEO. So-called gaffer, big boss man.

So here he was, sitting in a car park in his best duds—cream cotton suit, white shirt and pointy-toed brown brogues—trying to get pictures of a cheating husband. Like in a film from the fifties. Pool of shite.

He put the camera on the floor and leaned back in the seat. Problems, problems and more fucking problems. He needed this malarkey like he needed a neat three-inch hole in the head. Two key operatives off on the sick. On the skive more likely. Or shagging each other. He laughed out loud. That would be something. Investigate that one. Watching the watchers. And what if he could prove they were swinging the lead? He could hardly sack them. He needed them. You couldn't just put an advert in the local paper for experienced surveillance operatives, could you? All sorts of dickheads, smackheads, and knobheads would apply. He needed to beef up the HR. And sort out the bad debts. Cope with all the changes in technology. Get new clients.

He moved across into the passenger seat, opened the door and slid out, the camera with its telephoto lens in one hand, then crept around the car and walked quickly into the trees. He worked his way round to the Merc, dodging from tree to tree. *Carry on spying.* There had to be a better way than this. Eventually he drew close to the car. Everything was still. Must've stopped for a breather. They were in the back seat. *In flagrante delicto.* Window so steamed up you couldn't work out what was going on inside.

He brought up the camera, edged forward and crouched down. Now he could see both faces. Got it. With the registration number, clear proof. He jogged back through the trees to his car, opened the passenger door, threw the camera in the back and squirmed into the driver's seat.

Well at least he'd accomplished something on this pool of shite day. He started up the engine and wound down the window. Sweat ran into his eyes. His head hurt.

A big, angry, pink-red face appeared only a foot away. The man from the Merc. Where had he come from! In his surprise, Jack let the window go all the way down.

'Fucking pervert snooper!' The man's face was as pink as a ham hanging in a butcher's shop. Jack could clearly see the big pores on his nose. 'Why don't you get a proper job? Picking up dog turds in this car park would be about your level. You people are the lowest of the low. In fact,' the face moved closer, 'you're like a big turd left steaming on the grass over there. How does it feel to be a big shitty dog turd?'

Jack opened his mouth to say something, point out that the 'shitty' adjective wasn't needed, but the man lowered his head and butted Jack hard on the bridge of his nose, striking with a loud thunk of bone on gristle. Pain. Blood. Silly thought: he'd let his guard down and fallen for a textbook 'Kirkby Kiss'. An experienced private investigator wouldn't have been caught out like this.

CHAPTER TWO

Jack had to tap on the reception desk before Lucy looked up from her computer.

She examined his face and smiled. 'What happened to your nose?' A fan on the desk ruffled her dark hair.

Jack thought for a moment. Might as well come clean. 'The subject of the surveillance wasn't happy about it,' he said.

He popped into the toilet and examined his face in the mirror. He'd only had to wait for ten minutes at the walk-in surgery. Quiet time. They'd glued the edges of the wound together with skin adhesives, which weren't really stitches. After three to five days they could just be peeled off. The plaster only partly covered the big, red bruise, and you could see where it was already going purple. And there were spots of blood on his suit jacket and white shirt. He managed to rub some of them away with his fingers, but you could still see the traces. The bleeding wouldn't stop. It was the tablets he was taking to thin the blood. Most men in their fifties seemed to be taking them and leaving trails of non-clotting blood wherever they went. He made a wedge with toilet tissue and carefully inserted it into the bleeding nostril. He took another wedge and stuffed it in his pocket.

Lucy was waiting for him when he came out. 'Look, Jack, we need to go over a few things.'

'Can't it wait? I'm meeting the new client any minute now.'

'It's important.'

'Okay, make it quick.'

For once the air-conditioning in the meeting room was working. In the cooler air he suddenly felt sick and faint. He sat down on one of the chairs arranged around the table with a thump.

'Are you okay?' Lucy asked. He nodded, and she sat on one of the chairs across the table from him and opened a file. 'Look; basically, we're going to go pop unless you do something.' She put her finger in the side of her mouth and made a loud popping noise, like a young kid.

Lucy, doubled, well, trebled, as the firm's receptionist, administrator and financial officer. And office manager. That made four. Quadrupled? Duh.

'Since we lost the council contract,' she said, 'we've been in trouble. Bills, cash flow, well, cash trickle; you name it. And now we've got this accreditation problem with the association. Only Mel is a member. And I can't see the likes of Roy going back to college, can you? We need some new clients.'

The bell on reception buzzed.

Jack tentatively eased the wedge of tissue out of his nostril. The bleeding seemed to have stopped. He eased the wedge back.

'Talking of potential new clients,' Lucy said, 'your visitor is here.'

*

His new client—well, hopefully his new client—was standing in reception and looking at Jack's Patrick Heron print. Orange and red. He'd picked it up on a dirty weekend to Newquay with one of his girlfriends; they'd ended up in The Tate.

'Sarah Gladwyn?' he said. 'Jack Gordon. Do you like it?' He nodded at the painting.

'Oh yes. We've got the original in our St Ives cottage. I love that kind of post war stuff they did in that area.'

Silence while he took this in.

'Sorry about being late,' he said at last. 'Slight accident in the car. This idiot pulled out, and I had to do an emergency stop.' He motioned at his nose. 'That's how I got this.'

'Sure it wasn't in the line of duty?' She smiled. 'You being a private detective?'

He laughed and led the way into the interview room, which had two comfortable armchairs, a low table, air conditioning and nice decor. And a nice painting. Impress clients and set them at ease. Starting with the nice painting in reception.

He motioned to the armchairs, and they sat down facing each other. Jack had grabbed a new casefile from reception, and he put this on the table.

They examined each other. He thought she must be in her mid-fifties but was very well preserved: dark-blue pin-stripe suit; short, blonde hair; well dressed—very well dressed. People with money wore clothes that fitted them, that looked right. His assessment of Sarah Gladwyn used the word 'very' a lot, he realised.

He smiled at her and leaned back. 'So how can I help you? Your name, Gladwyn. It sounds familiar.' He opened the file and pulled out a checklist sheet.

She nodded. 'My husband, Oliver Gladwyn, is in the news at the moment.'

'The vegan chap who owns Wirral Wanderers?' Jack suppressed a laugh. 'Isn't he the feller behind the new Liverpool barrage? Haven't they got some new proposals to save the scheme?'

She nodded again. 'He's presenting them at the Riverside Conference Centre on Wednesday.' She paused. 'We're an old family. North Wales, though we did have a house in Liverpool until a few years ago. You might think being from an old family was a curse to read some of the stuff we've been receiving. That's why I'm here.'

'Threatening stuff?'

She nodded. 'Letters, e-mails, tweets. Always signed by "The Ferret: Prodigal Son of Glyndwr".'

He laughed and made a note on the checklist. 'What like those Welsh nationalists who used to burn down houses and blow up dams in the sixties?'

She nodded. 'They call themselves anarchists now, Mr Gordon. My family was a major landowner in North Wales until recently. Farms, slate quarries, reservoirs. We were blamed for many things. Whether they were true or not, people still bear grudges.'

He nodded. 'Okay. Do you have any examples of these threats?'

She handed over a file.

He leafed through the letters and printouts of emails. 'Have you been to the police?'

'Naturally. They investigated, but they couldn't identify anyone. The letters are typed up and printed off in various internet cafes—those are photocopies by the way. The emails are sent from the same places. The police say the anarchist community is a closed one, like a resistance movement. They cover each other's backs, move between safe houses, that kind of thing. Whoever this is covers his tracks well ...'

'His? It could be a her. Let's not be sexist.' A little bit of cheek back.

She smiled at him before turning away—in that moment he caught a clear view of her eyes— green, like the sea when you dive deep. 'Of course.'

'So why did you come to us?'

'I'd heard that, while you are somewhat unconventional, you get results.'

He flicked through the letters and stopped at one. He read it aloud: 'We know all your secrets, Gladwyn filth. The quarrymen who died on the job or starved during the strikes. The villages cleared for English reservoirs. The slaves who died on your plantations. The skeletons in your cupboard. The innocent girls sacrificed on the altars of your lust. Retribution is coming ...'

Jack looked up. 'Is there any truth in these accusations?'

She shrugged. 'Some of it. I'm not my brother's keeper, and neither am I my ancestors' keeper. How could I be? Most old families have stuff like this in their history. Most made their money from compensation for stopping trading in slaves. Did you know that?'

'Well, I knew that Liverpool was built on the bones of slaves ...' He looked back to the letter and read on. 'And we know the truth about your latest escapade. Building a dam across the Mersey to make lots of money for you and your cronies when solar and wind power would be better for the planet.' He laughed. 'So they're green warriors as well now? Probably just some lonely geek tapping away at his troll posts in the back bedroom of his mother's house.'

'Except they vandalised one of our cars. Painted graffiti on it.' She lifted her bag, rooted in it and handed over a photo.

A top of the range Mercedes, light blue. Surprise, surprise. It would hardly have been a clapped-out Ford Focus, would it? Bright-red letters painted across the bonnet read 'Gladwyn shite'. He noticed several dents and punctures, and a splintered hole in the windscreen.

Neither said anything for a few moments.

'And the skeletons in the cupboard?' he said. 'Innocent girls sacrificed on the altars of your lust?'

She sighed and made a dismissive move with her hand. 'I think that refers to my sister, Helen,' she said. 'She disappeared many years ago. Suicide. Supposedly.'

'Supposedly? I take it you don't agree with the verdict?'

She shrugged. 'It was thirty-five years ago: 1983. What could we do now?'

'Hmm. It wouldn't even be considered a cold case after that long. More a dead one. Sorry.'

'It's okay. There's one more thing. My husband has a colleague. John Puller. Pals going way back. He has some sort of hold over Oliver. His firm was recently given a partnership deal to develop land associated with the barrage. Out of the blue. No discussion, nothing.'

Jack sat thinking for a moment then gathered all the papers together.

'Okay, we can have a look at this for you, Mrs Gladwyn.' We? It would probably be himself in the current staffing crisis. 'Our standard rates and expenses are explained in our information pack. We'll invoice you every week starting this Friday. We prefer payment by bank transfer.'

She nodded.

He lifted the phone. 'Lucy, could you let Mrs Gladwyn have a client's information pack and contract on the way out?' He looked up. 'If you could carefully read then sign both copies of the contract in the pack, Mrs Gladwyn, keep one and send the other back to us in the envelope provided. We'll get onto this right away—could we photocopy those letters before you leave?—and we'll give you a written update by email in a week's time ...' He gingerly pulled at the wedge of tissue in his nostril. Surely it had clotted by now? No; a fountain of bright red blood rewarded him. He had to quickly move his head to avoid contaminating the evidence.

'Just one thing, Mr Gordon.'

He pressed the wedge of tissue against his nose. 'Yes?'

'I want my husband to be kept out of this investigation. Please don't contact him. He has enough on his plate at the moment. Please do everything through me. I want this to be a discreet, sensitive, low-key operation with the police kept out of it if at all possible.'

CHAPTER THREE

'Your other visitor's here.' Lucy didn't look up from her screen. Was she playing a game? Or chatting to a friend on Facebook or something?

'My other one? What other one?'

'Stuart Madison from the National Crime Agency. He rang up on the off chance. Apparently, it's super-urgent. He's waiting in the cafe.'

The cafe was three shops along the parade, past a bookie and an empty unit with the shutter down. Stuart sat outside at the only table. It was out of the sun and had a parasol above it; thank god. He was by himself. No doubt the spot chosen because no one could listen in. Stuart was in his early thirties now, and his spiky hairstyle was becoming more subdued. He wore a blue suit and a white, open-necked shirt—the lack of a tie an obvious rebellion against convention.

'Ah, Jack,' he said when Jack sat down with his coffee. 'I like coming here to see you. The coffee's shite and the view's awful. Whatever happened to your nose?' They each took a sip of their drink. 'Looks painful.'

'I had an argument with a swing door going into Kentucky Fried Chicken.' Jack didn't say that prior notice of Stuart's visit would've been polite. The NCA were a good intermittent source of work. It had taken several years and lots of hurdle-jumping to get on their select list of trusted security contractors.

'It's nice to see you, Stuart,' Jack continued. 'How are things going with the organised crime scene? Had any good shoot-outs lately?'

Stuart sighed. 'Taking a back seat at the moment. The priority is this international terrorism.'

'What? ISIS and all that?'

'And all that.' He winced as if someone had poked him with something sharp. 'We've got it under control, but it's a manpower drain. To be honest, we've reached a dead end and so have the police. Everyone can spot a plain-clothes plod these days. I don't know what methods you use, and I don't want to know what methods you use, just so long as you get results. That's where you can help us, Jack.'

'Be glad to.' He mustn't give any inkling of the present staffing crisis. 'How can we be of help?'

'We've got intelligence that a new group is infiltrating the country. Using Western, European-looking people so as not to attract attention.'

'What? Wearing pin-stripe suits and bowlers and carrying brollies?'

'More like football shirts, baggy shorts, trainers and wearing baseball caps back to front. No, look, there was this militant group in the Atlas Mountains of Morocco, Ansar Dine. They started off fighting for home rule from Morocco. Recently they've affiliated with ISIS and declared war on the West. The intelligence is that they aim to infiltrate one of our big cities and contaminate the water supply. Cause mass panic. The code word is *Aman Iman*: Water is Life.'

Jack laughed. '*Aman Iman*? What? Like that Arab rock group? What are they called?'

Stuart grimaced. '*Tinariwen*. And they're not Arabs, they're Tuaregs. We've got no evidence that the band are involved. But this shower has taken over some of the buzz words. Look, the brief is to keep a low profile, ask around and feed anything you get back to us.'

Jack thought. 'I dunno, Stuart. These ethnic groups—Pakistanis, Somalis—they stick together, distrust outsiders ...'

'I know, but the word is that they're using proxies who look and sound like Westerners—Chechens, Turks, anarchists, people like that. Just keep your ears to the rails. Here's a copy of the dossier. Keep it locked away.'

'Do we know what sort of poison?'

Stuart shrugged. 'Sarin. Arsenic, anthrax, botulism, take your pick. Probably genetically modified. All we can be certain of is that it will be tasteless, colourless and won't be broken down quickly. And it won't be LSD; that doesn't work.'

'It's a bit obvious, though, contaminating the water supply. Haven't the authorities thought of that and put measures in place?'

'Well, yes. But each big urban area includes lots of small reservoirs, all linked together by water pipes. The utilities don't have the manpower to watch everything. They have CCTV and door keypads in place, but that doesn't solve anything.'

'Rather. Every scally eight-year-old knows how to watch cameras and avoid getting their mugs photographed. We used to have a tape showing a ladder appearing, then two hands unscrewing the camera.'

'Exactly, so we need a bit of left-field thinking.' Stuart paused. He suddenly looked very young for the job. More like a fresh-faced fourteen-year-old than a grown man. 'Look, Jack,' he said. 'I won't beat about the bush. We're stumped on this. Anyone we could send in would stand out like a bright-pink bellend. You and your team know the ground, you blend in. You did a great job on that Malone case, for instance.'

Jack said nothing. That one had been a fluke. Roy had overheard a conversation in a pub between a group of middle-aged men who seemed like your standard posse of workmates having a pint after work but were in fact the most violent gangsters in Liverpool. Trouble was, they were all out of jail now or about to be released. And they might be looking to settle a few scores.

'Standard consultancy rates and expenses?' Jack said.

Stuart nodded. 'Just invoice us at the end of each calendar month. He pushed back his cup and saucer and stood up.

When he'd gone, Jack closed his eyes and leaned back in his chair. Two big jobs in one morning. This was the opportunity to put things right. But first he needed some staff. He opened his eyes and snapped to attention in his chair.

CHAPTER FOUR

Roy Hannon lived in West Derby, once a little village but swallowed up by Liverpool a long time ago. More like a Lancashire town than Liverpool, with lots of those little red-brick terraced houses you find in Burnley or Bolton.

Roy's house was in one of those terraces. No reply to Jack's knocking, and curtains pulled. Roy was divorced and virtually lived in the pub, but it was a little too early for that. Jack walked around the back. The alley had the security gates that seemed to be standard across the city. Just as Jack was about to give it up as a bad job, the gate opened and an old lady pulled out a wheelie bin.

'Morning,' Jack said cheerfully, trusting to his suit and tie to remove any suspicion that he was a burglar. So long as she didn't notice the half-rubbed-out blood spots. And the big plaster on his nose might raise suspicion. She didn't notice, just shrugged and let him past. Number eleven. He counted along the properties. The yard door was unlocked. Rubbish, rubble, an old washing machine and a rusting fridge. Jack tried the back door—also unlocked. Inside the atmosphere was warm and fusty, all the windows shut, and an awful smell hit him: a mixture of sweaty feet, boiled cabbage and rotten food. Jack just stopped himself from throwing up.

Roy lay asleep on a sofa in the front room, wrapped in a blanket. Jack pulled the curtains, dragged a chair over and sat down. He examined Roy's face in the harsh light: grey skin; grey hair; two days' worth of grey stubble; dark, swollen patches under the eyes; skin like the landscape of a mountainous area seen from space, mainly grey with yellow and red blotches, the surface of a volcanic Jovian moon; mouth open, revealing an amazing display that could've been used by a dentist to demonstrate what happens to your teeth if you never brush them, live on chips and chain-smoke roll-ups. Lines and creases; fifty years old, looks more like sixty. His liver, the seat of life, had packed in, and he'd been turned down for a transplant. Couldn't keep off the pop. And he was physically shrinking—when driving his car, he sat so low in the seat that it looked as if no-one was driving. But he was an invaluable member of staff: knew everyone in the Liverpool underworld; lived in pubs, sitting at the bar, chatting and listening in to conversations.

Surprisingly, he also knew his way around a computer.

Jack shook his shoulder. No response. He punched the shoulder hard.

An eye opened, yellow and bloodshot. 'Well, whaddaya know if it isn't Flash fucking Gordon himself.'

'What the ...!' Jack recoiled from the blast of bad breath.

'Jumping Jack Flash more like,' Roy said, calm as anything. 'How'd you get the nose —flashing in the park?'

Jack couldn't stop himself from retorting to this. 'Let's have a little bit of respect, Hannon. After all, I am your boss. Remember? The mug who puts food on your table. I got this nose in the line of duty, filling in for staff who've gone AWOL. In the army you'd be shot for talking like that.'

Hannon pulled the blanket over his head. 'Oh, fuck off and leave me alone,' came his muffled voice. 'I've had enough of it all.'

'Had enough of what?'

'This. Life.'

Jack thought for a while. 'Come on, Roy,' he said at last. 'I need you for a job.'

The blanket came down to reveal a pair of yellow eyes that had strings of blood in them like fertilised egg yolks.

'Oh, sorry, Mr Gordon. What ...?'

'I thought you had the flu. Sure it's not the aftereffects of a bender?'

Roy sat up. 'I was sure it was the flu.'

Jack went into the kitchen and put the kettle on. He found a glass—dirty, of course—washed it, filled it with water and took it in.

Roy drank greedily.

'Roy,' Jack said. 'I need you for an important job.'

'But I've got the flu.'

'You've not got the flu; you've got the mother of all hangovers.'

'I've not got a hangover. I just had a quick six ... well six in each pub.'

Jack waved away Hannon's pleas. 'I could sack you here and now, but I need you, unfortunately. We've got two big jobs. Anarchists harassing this posh family in Wales, and Islamic terrorists plotting to plant stuff in Liverpool's water supply.'

'Anarchists and terrorists? Won't see much of them in the usual watering holes. And Liverpool could do with something in its water supply. Cut down the robbing and the drug-taking ...'

Well, I've not heard that one from you before, Jack thought. *Best ignore it.*

'There's a bonus in it if you come up with the goods,' Jack said. 'I'll make you some tea and some food. And that's where you're wrong, Mr Hannon. Islamic terrorists are now using Western-looking people who go in pubs. Exactly where the plods won't look. And anarchists might like a pint, for Chrissake. Have you got a shower?'

Roy shook his head. 'It's broken. I've been trying to get a plumber but ...'

Jack checked the kitchen: overflowing rubbish bin; the remains of takeaway chip shop meals spread over the work surface and the floor; sink overflowing with grey, greasy water and filthy dishes and pans. Nothing new there, then. Fridge empty apart from a couple of cans of Heineken. And an egg. One egg.

'I'm just popping out to the corner shop,' Jack shouted.

Five minutes later he arrived back with a carrier bag bulging with basics: bread, butter, tea, milk. Roy was gone. Jack loaded the stuff into the fridge and set off. He knew where Roy would be.

The greasy spoon cafe was in a parade of shops on the main road a few hundred yards away. It was deserted, apart from Roy, who was dressed in a scruffy tracksuit—not one of his natty outfits; it was too early for the pub. He was tucking into a big breakfast of sausage, egg, bacon, beans, fried bread and black pudding. It made Jack sick just to look at it and smell the grease, but he got himself a black coffee and joined Roy.

'Sorry, mate,' Roy said. He harpooned a sausage and stuffed it into his mouth. Jack had to turn away as Roy spoke with his mouth full. 'Best cure for a hangover—line the stomach with grease.'

'Don't your ex clients remember you when you're in the pub—the ones you put away. I'd have thought that they might want to settle old scores.'

'Occasionally. But most are still in jail or dead, and my appearance, let's face it, has changed somewhat. I used to be a handsome man, if you remember. Before the death sentence.'

'Death sentence, bollocks. Give up the pop and the grease and you'll be fit in no time.'

'Nah. The sawbones tried to tell me that, but it's too late. He asked me if I was a moderate drinker—you know like everyone lies about it. "No," I said, "I'm a heavy drinker—could you note that down. *Heavy drinker.*"' He spelled out the letters. 'Besides, I know the score. I checked it up on the internet. Liver cancer is a death sentence cos it just spreads throughout the body.'

Roy tackled the last of the grub, mopping up the grease, egg yolk and tomato sauce with a piece of fried bread. When he'd finished, he pushed the plate away and let out a loud belch.

'But you didn't have this condition when you were pensioned off, did you?' Jack said.

'Nah, early retirement. They wanted to get rid of both of us, didn't they? You got out on the bleeding-heart nervous breakdown scam.'

'You reckon?' Don't rise to the bait. Act daft. 'Why would they want to get rid of us?'

'Don't pretend you don't know. Sitting there with that expression on your face. Pumping me for information. Them shenanigans with Mick Malone and Puller and Whitaker went right to the top. That poor girl didn't drown herself—everyone knows that. They wanted to get rid of anyone who might ask questions and poke around. We're both best out of it.'

'Okay,' Jack said eventually. 'You just finish your grease and your tea, and we'll get over to the office. We've got work to do'

CHAPTER FIVE

Jack parked up opposite Mel's house. Her place was a modern, mock-Tudor detached house on the edge of Widnes—manicured lawns; the odd reasonably new car parked up; streets deserted at mid-morning. It would've been worth a lot more in a better area, though it was nice enough. On the salary Jack paid her, and as a single mother, it would be difficult enough to pay the mortgage and all the other bills. And, as far as Jack knew, she had no other source of income. Her own business had gone pop, and she'd been declared bankrupt. It must have taken some organising with the mortgage company and the utilities to keep things going as before. Still, it was none of his business. She was good at her job— tenacious, cool-headed and experienced—and that was that mattered. She was particularly good at keeping up with advances in technology; her mastery of social media was just one example.

He got out of the car, walked up the path and rang the bell.

'What the fuck happened to you?' she said when she opened the door.

Without make-up, her blonde hair tied back and in a shapeless dressing gown, Mel Gibson looked older than her early forties. Jack preferred her like this, much more than when she was all dolled up.

Inside the house felt nice and cool. The blinds were closed, and a big fan purred on the ceiling. For a moment, he toyed with the idea of making a pass. Her bed would be nice and warm. But she'd only smack him in the face, open the cut on his nose and give him a black eye. If not two black eyes. She'd made herself clear when he'd tried it on not long after she started working for him.

'On yer bike, lar,' she'd said then. 'If you were my type, Jack, I'd take you up on that. But you look like an ageing Elvis impersonator. By all accounts you were a ladies' man once, but now you're past it, mate.'

Fair enough, he'd thought. The truth isn't slander.

Now he was getting tired of explaining about the nose. 'Morgan,' he said, following her in. 'Kirkby Kiss. I'd have given him ten out of ten for execution.'

'Oh, Jack, I am sorry. I didn't think he'd go that far. Bastard. It was a chance to box that case off. I had to stay at home. Harriet said she was ill. Though I'm not so sure now.'

'Mo-o-m,' came a voice from upstairs. 'I'm hungry!'

'See what I mean?'

'Anyway, I got the pictures. Bum in the air, the lot.'

She giggled. 'Look, come and sit down. That looks painful. Would you like a cuppa?'

'Never thought you'd ask.'

He watched her make the coffee, then they carried their mugs into the front room—real oak flooring; walls painted magnolia; nice paintings, real ones, a variety of oils, water colours, portraits and country scenes. Her own work?

'Look, Mel,' he said, once they'd sat down, he on the sofa, her on an armchair, 'You know I wouldn't bother you at home if it wasn't important ...'

'It's okay, Jack, I know you're one of life's gentlemen.'

He smiled. 'We've got a couple of big jobs that have suddenly come up. I need all hands-on deck. Can you sort out Harriet and help me out? Leave the honey-potting for a while?'

She thought. 'I'll manage.' Pause. 'That looks really painful.'

'I've had worse.'

She laughed. 'So have I. We've both had a lot worse.' She paused as if expecting him to say something. 'Don't want to talk about it?' she said. 'I can understand that.'

'You've never told me all there is to know about your own problems.'

She laughed. 'We'll have to get drunk some time and cry on each other's shoulders.'

'Who was the father?'

'Don't beat about the bush, do you?' She laughed. 'I hear that you've got a few secrets tucked away yourself.'

He grinned. 'It's not a secret. I've been unlucky in love a few times.'

'Unlucky? Leaving the poor girl with the baby. In my book that makes you the villain.'

'It's not as simple as that, Mel, you know that. If a woman takes a downer on you and won't give you access to a kid, that doesn't make you a villain. Especially as she has no problem accepting the standing order every month. So what happened to the daddy in your case?'

'Charlie? Oh, he's a psychopath from central casting. Does everything he can to avoid paying the monthly cheque. Changes addresses, jobs, girlfriends. They can't track him down. He used to occasionally take the notion to track me down. Bit ironic, really. Seeing as it's my job to track people down.'

Jack noticed her use of the past tense when she referred to her ex-partner trying to track her down. He nodded at a framed photo of Harriet on the mantelpiece.

'I can see a lot of you in her, but there's something else.'

'What? Nastiness? Maybe that's where she gets it from. Not nastiness, awkwardness.' She paused. 'Yes,' she said in response to Jack's quizzical look. 'She likes her toast burned. Won't eat it otherwise. Don't ask me. She's going through a phase. Like adolescence but before. She's always in trouble at school—always messing about in class.'

'Maybe you're too indulgent ... Burnt toast?' Jack shrugged.

'You mean I've spoilt her.'

'Probably. I knew a boy at junior school, George Durant. He was spoiled rotten. Fat as a beach ball. Lived on a diet of chocolate and cakes. His parents used to take George and me out to the country in this big, old black Morris Oxford. Leather seats. Old man Durant had a big beak of a nose like a vulture.' He laughed. 'Anyway, at school young George used to say horrible things to the other kids. He didn't realise, of course, that in life you reap what you sow. I went around to his house once. I think his parents wanted him to have some friends. They owned an electrical shop—plugs, light bulbs, that kind of thing. They were quite well off. It was okay for a while, but then he went into a violent tantrum over nothing. I had to go home. We went to separate secondary schools, and I heard later that he'd had to be taken out because he was bullied so much.'

Jack didn't mention the time years later when he'd passed the same shop with its sign reading *Durant Electricals* and glanced in: so shabby and dusty;

yellowing electrical parts; greying signs. Obviously finding it hard to compete with B&Q nearby, where you could buy your electric plugs and fuses cheaper. And behind the counter sat George Durant. Not fat anymore but exactly like his dad—gaunt; a huge vulture's beak of a nose; yellow skin; balding skull. He stared into space, not noticing Jack, who gaped for a moment and then turned away.

Mel took a swig of tea. 'Now what are these two jobs?'

'Mu-u-um!' The voice came from up the stairs, more insistent this time. 'I'm hungry! You know I don't like toast like this. I like it burned!'

CHAPTER SIX

Jack googled *Gladwyn family North Wales*, notebook and the photocopies of the letters at the ready. His office was nice and cool, just right for getting some work done. He needed to run a first check of his notes of the meeting with Sarah Gladwyn. Wikipedia was the usual first step; the references at the end of a Wikipedia article often led to the real nuggets of information.

Richard Gladwyn was a rich Liverpool merchant who made his pile from the Jamaica slaves and sugar trade. Slaves in, sugar out. In 1780 he married and built Aigburth Hall. Jack noted this and added *It's the one!* underlining the words. Gladwyn soon moved to North Wales where he set up the slate industry and, with the profits from this and the slave/sugar trade, built a huge picturesque castle called Gladwyn Castle. He was raised to the peerage as Lord Gladwyn. The slate industry was an unforgiving one for the workers, with high rates of injury and death. The resentment against this and low wages caused the strikes of 1900 to 1903 when families virtually starved to death. And then in the 1960s the then Lord Gladwyn, Sarah's father, sold huge areas of land to the Manchester and Liverpool corporations to build reservoirs, causing several traditional Welsh communities to be moved against their will. The Gladwyns moved permanently to North Wales and sold off the Liverpool house in the early 1980s when their daughter Helen (Sarah's sister) disappeared in tragic circumstances—a presumed suicide by drowning. Was this one of those 'skeletons in the cupboard' referred to in the threatening letter?

So Freddie the stalker was right to some degree. The Gladwyns had much to feel guilty for— if they were capable of such an emotion as guilt. Oliver Gladwyn was the latest in the lineage; he married into the family and changed his name to become the latest Lord Gladwyn—his previous name had been Oliver Rutter.

Jack opened a new page in his notebook and googled *Oliver Gladwyn*. Page after page of newspaper and magazine articles overwhelmed him: darling of the alternative culture; bought Wirral Wanderers and forced players to throw away the bacon butties and pork pies and become vegans; installed solar panels on the roof of the stand; and then the proposed barrage, the answer to climate change. But there seemed to be a problem with financing. Jack would've thought the prospect of energy from the waves would be attractive, but the big up-front capital cost and the years of loan repayments was a problem. Jack checked the images for Oliver Gladwyn and found a big, beaming face with a friendly expression framed by a monster mullet.

He googled *Oliver Rutter*. Ahh, now this was where the nuggets would be. He dropped out from an engineering course at Birmingham University, so obviously not dumb. A former traveller, now married with two kids, he was arrested in the mid-1990s in Australia on charges of drug smuggling with J. Puller. The name seemed familiar. Jack made a note. *Big trial. Found not guilty.*

Jack read through the sheaf of photocopied emails from Sarah again. He googled *Freddie the Ferret*. Again, a landslide of articles. Freddie the Ferret was the leader of a group of anarchists who had terrorised establishment targets in the Bristol area—police stations, the homes of Tory politicians, newspaper offices. He'd evaded capture up to now mainly because of an organisation of fellow anarchists and sympathisers. His father was a Welsh activist, one of the founders of the Sons of Glyndwr who fought against the building of dams in the sixties. Caught and imprisoned after a failed attempt to blow up a water pipeline in Cheshire, he committed suicide in prison. So Freddie had a beef against the Gladwyns.

Jack scrolled through until he found a photo. It showed a man with glasses, long hair at the back, bald at the front, like Bill Bailey the comedian. The photo was a bit fuzzy, but the face looked familiar. Jack couldn't quite place it.

Heavy metal music started in the flat next door, the sound thumping through the wall. It always started around ten o'clock in the morning when the occupants got up—presumably they didn't have jobs. Jack closed the screen and pushed the notebook away. The constant noise and the smell from the chippy on the other side made it difficult to project any kind of image for Jack's business. He'd done his best with the decor, but the location was obviously down market. He would've liked a nice modern office unit on a leafy business park on the edge of the city, but he couldn't afford it.

A chip shop, a bookie, a cafe and Jack's business occupied the shopping parade. Two shop units sat empty, with steel roller shutters covered in flyers and graffiti. The flat above Jack's unit had been converted into meeting rooms and offices, the one over the chip shop was empty, and the unseen heavy metal head bangers occupied the flat on the other side.

Jack found the smell of cooking chips the worst thing. Chin, a Liverpudlian of Chinese descent, ran the chippie. He was always courteous when Jack approached him, but only shrugged if Jack mentioned the smell. 'What can I do?' he'd say in his scouse accent. In the heat he had to open all the windows or the fryers would be literally cooked alive. They couldn't afford to change the oil every five minutes, and they couldn't afford extraction equipment. Jack could imagine what it'd be like to fry chips all day in this heat with no air conditioning, so he always let the matter drop.

Roy had related the story circulating the local pub: a local lady had worked there for a while and had cleared some well-out-of-date sausages, fluorescent with blue mould, out of the fridge and into the bin. Later that night she noticed the sausages going into the fryer, obviously retrieved from the bin. Jack, Lucy and Mel avoided the chippy after that, but Roy tucked into the takeaways from there with relish—especially enjoying the sausage suppers.

'Come on now, concentrate on Freddie!' Jack said out loud.

He read through his notes. It would be difficult to track down Freddie Devon if an anarchist community with tight security protected him—safe houses and all that rigmarole. But two snippets of information piqued Jack's interest: Helen Gladwyn had committed suicide not long after Oliver Rutter had become Oliver Gladwyn and been accepted by the Gladwyn family; and Oliver had been arrested and put on trial in a drug smuggling case with Johnny Puller as his co-defendant. They'd got off. Case dismissed for lack of evidence.

He closed the notebook and leaned back in his chair. J. Puller. John Puller. Johnny Puller.

CHAPTER SEVEN

'Shouldn't our insurance be beefed up with the level of threat we're getting these days?' Roy said. 'We've all been threatened recently, haven't we? And we've had graffiti daubed all over the shop front. *SS snoopers fuck off.* Charming.'

Jack stifled a sigh. Roy was at his most self-righteous—he always seemed to be on edge when he wasn't in the pub—and he was wearing one of his pub outfits: light-grey sports jacket and black trousers, dark-brown brogues, open-necked white shirt, shaved, hair combed.

He had several other outfits, all kept carefully clean and ironed, based on different jackets, trousers and suits. The clothes were getting a little frayed at the edges, but the impression he gave was always of the well-off gent. The house might be a tip, but he put on a show when going out. The local greasy spoon café didn't count as 'out', and once 'out' he put on the persona of the 'gent about town', entering into amicable conversations with strangers in pubs. Trouble was, the mask could slip, and the misogynistic old git be let out.

Today Roy was obviously in a bad mood. The air conditioning was on the blink again and everyone was tired, listless and tetchy with the heat.

'And ...' A big smirk broke out on Roy's stupid face. 'Mr Gordon gets a Kirkby Kiss when he's on a job. Not on the job. That was the subject of the surveillance.'

Someone began to titter then stopped. Jack tried to control himself and not react to yet another of Roy's insinuations. He looked around at the typical meeting room: grey carpet, magnolia-painted walls, and oak-veneer table, the ends peeling away where idiots had picked at the edges. He made a mental note to investigate getting the room re-decorated and getting a new air-conditioning system. Jack got up, walked to the window and opened it as far as it would go. All it did was let in a blast of cooking chips and the thump-thump of heavy metal.

'I like mine crisp, not soggy,' Roy said with a straight face. 'And with lots of salt and vinegar. Oh, and hold the Motörhead.' He nodded at the wall. 'Couldn't we get them out of there or something? Fucking noisy neighbours!'

'In fact,' Lucy said, coming to Jack's assistance. 'That's one of the issues raised by the association. We need to sort it out. To keep our accreditation and our professional indemnity insurance.'

Everyone looked at her with blank faces.

'To cater for the threats we meet in our line of work,' she said. 'And,' she stood up and approached the whiteboard, 'in addition to qualifications and insurance, we need to sort out ...' she pointed at the list, 'bad debt, recruiting procedures, staff contracts, pensions, sickness, new technology ... In fact, we need to look at human resources generally.'

'Human resources?' Roy scoffed. 'What's wrong with good old personnel matters.?

'I know you're a luddite, Roy,' Lucy said, a half smile on her face. 'But we've got to move with the times. We're a medium-sized business now, and we must get all this sorted. Otherwise we go under.' She paused. '*Comprendez!*' she added with a sharper tone. 'This business is changing. As Mr Gordon will explain shortly, we are in financial trouble because the private investigation world is changing. Honey-trapping and benefit fraud aren't enough anymore. We've got to change with it or go under. Jack has some good news, and we've got to take advantage of new opportunities and turn things around.' She paused for effect, then continued, 'Jack? It's all yours.'

'Jobs in this game,' Jack said, 'are like buses; nothing for ages then ten come along at once. Well, in this case, two.' He went to the whiteboard and rubbed out Lucy's list. 'First the Gladwyns.' He wrote the name on the board. 'Old Liverpool family. Made their money in the rum, sugar and slave trade, then moved to Wales.'

'Where they moved on,' Roy said, 'from slaves to exploiting the local Welshies.'

Jack laughed. 'How did you know that?'

'It's common knowledge. I had a gran who lived near Llanberis. They extracted slate, left loads of quarrymen dead or crippled for life, then they flooded the valleys and sold the water to the English.'

Jack passed his hand over his head. 'You obviously know more about it than me, Roy. Maybe you should be up here doing the briefing.'

'No, you carry on. We're not here to pass moral judgement on our clients. We're here to earn a living.'

'And don't forget,' Jack said, 'all this is historical. The present members of the family can't be held to account for what their ancestors did. Though some people seem to think that they should. Like this anarchist group that have been threatening the family.' He wrote *Anarchists* on the board. Seems Oliver Gladwyn,' he added the name to the board, 'the latest lord, is behind the plans to build a barrage on the Mersey. For some reason the anarchists don't like it; they want wind farms. I would've thought that it was about as clean as you can get but ...'

He shrugged and made a motion with a hand. 'Seems like the family have lost faith in the police,' he continued. 'They want to try a more unconventional approach. Lucy's compiled a file which will be kept in room four under lock and key. No copying of documents, okay? Which brings me to the second job—for which we'll also keep a file in room four. I've done the initial internet trawl for each job.' He wrote *Islamic terrorists threaten Liverpool water supply* on the board. 'This is an NCA job. Again, they and the police have drawn a blank. This group is a more professional version of the usual Islamic terrorism pursued by a group of kids radicalised on the internet and who are in danger of blowing themselves up. No, this has been a long time in the planning. They use Western-looking people who go into the pubs and don't look or act like Arabs or whatever.'

Jack turned to face his audience, who were now concentrating on his or her thoughts. 'So what I'm suggesting is that Roy takes on the Islamic terrorism job and Mel the Gladwyn job.' He held up a hand. 'All notes and leads to be shared. The first obvious thing is to keep in mind that the two might be connected. It takes a bit of twisted thinking, but it's not beyond the bounds of possibility that anarchists might be connected to Islamists. It's possible. Try the obvious stuff first. Trawl the internet. Mel, set up fake Facebook profiles.' He looked at Roy. 'I can just see you pretending to be an Islamist.'

Roy laughed. 'And Mel an anarchist.'

'Roy,' Jack said. 'When was the last time you checked for bugs in this building?'

'Last week.'

'Well do it again straight after this meeting and reset our anti-hacking system.' He paused and grinned. 'And officially I've not said this, but, Roy, check all the usual databases.' He clapped his hands. 'Get to it everyone. This is our big opportunity! I obviously can't work undercover with my face in this state, so I'm relying on you.'

A titter went around the room.

'Mark of Cain,' someone whispered. Roy? Jack ignored it. He suddenly felt sick at the smell of cooking chips. What about a fan? One of those big ceiling fans? That might do the trick. He'd have to check the local Homebase. Or had they closed down?

CHAPTER EIGHT

Every time he nodded off, he returned to the dream. Now he was interacting with the girl, holding her hand, stroking her arm, talking quietly to each other, as if they were lovers. All this was silly. He hadn't been attracted to the girl, hardly knew her. And then at a certain stage in the dream, she began to whisper in his ear, repeating over and over, 'Help me, Jack. Help me.' Her refrain grew more and more plaintive and heart-rending until he had to force himself out of the dream and lie there terrified and shaking, his body covered in sweat and the sheets damp and twisted like ropes around his body.

The window was wide open, the curtains fluttering occasionally in a slight breeze, but it was still too hot to sleep. Should he go back for therapy? This was wearing him out. He needed sleep. Several bottles of beer and glasses of wine should've done the trick, but no. And the chip shop takeaway wouldn't have helped—fucking his guts up. He needed to start making his own meals with natural ingredients. And cut down on the pop. He checked the time: two o'clock.

A car went by on the Dock Road. As if in response, a ship's horn sounded far away on the river. He got up, showered and dressed, then sat for a while on the sofa in the living room, his mind blank. His nose had stopped bleeding at last, though it still ached, and his white shirt was steeping in cold water to try and get the bloodstains out. His cream suit would have to be dry-cleaned. What a mess.

And he was a mess: too many takeaways; not enough fruit and veg. He'd have to fit in a trip to the supermarket. What a drag.

He put on one of his videos, a nineteen fifties black-and-white Western, the ones he preferred: *Shane, High Noon, Gunfight at the O.K. Corral, Lonely are the Brave*—Frankie Laine cracking the whip and rasping out the lyrics. When he was a kid, he'd had to go to his aunties to watch *Rawhide*—his dad wouldn't let him watch TV after seven o'clock. He had a particular liking for Rowdy Yates played by Clint Eastwood before he was famous. His persona in the series had been so amiable that his rebranding as a cold-blooded killer was difficult to understand. 'Git three coffins ready.' Blam! Blam! Blam! Blam! 'My mistake, make that four.' Maybe it was precisely that amiability, like Alan Ladd's in *Shane*, that made the effect so convincing.

This time it was *3.10 to Yuma*.

'There's a lonely train, called the 3.10 to Yuma,' Frankie crooned, all soft before the whip-cracking bits.

Jack fast forwarded it through the slower bits, lingering on the scenes in which Evans's wife, played by Leora Dana, appeared. Now she was a real woman—and a real actress. These black-and-white Westerns from the Fifties always had real women as heroines, women with shapely bodies—usually wearing surprisingly tight clothes for the time. And the films always had a real story—in this one a marriage in crisis and a conflicted, desperate hero. Unlike John Wayne or Clint Eastwood who just played themselves.

The film closed with the breaking of the rains and the hero waving to his wife who sits in a buggy by the passing train. What an ending! It always made him feel good.

Jack rose and walked down the stairs. The security man looked up, surprised, from his book. What was his name? Harry? He was in his fifties, probably, thick-set with grey hair arranged in a spiky mullet—most likely he'd been a punk rocker in his teens and had kept the hairstyle. He was very nosey—in fact he had a huge beak of a nose—but that was a good thing for a security guard. Sitting in his little office by the entrance, with windows on three sides, he always kept an eye on his CCTV monitor: nothing escaped his attention.

CCTV was great if there was someone with half a brain monitoring it. Not so good when the person slept for most of the shift or watched porn movies. Jack had once surprised him and noted how quickly he changed what was on the screen.

'Just going for a walk, Barry,' he said.

'It's Harry, Mr Gordon,' the man said, stifling a smile.

Jack wondered if he'd made the same mistake with the name before. Maybe he was losing his marbles himself. 'Sorry, Harry,' he said. 'Can't sleep. Need some fresh air. Any action?'

Jack relied on Harry to keep an eye on things. It was quite ironic really. The watcher watching out for watchers. But there were people trying to track Jack down, no doubt about it. Which was why he rented out places for a short time before moving on. He'd been in this place for a few months, and it was time for a change, but the lodge wasn't ready. The good thing was that being within walking distance of scally areas meant that the security in this place had to be spot on.

Harry nodded and went back to his reading. He was obviously used to people coming and going at strange times. If Jack needed to smuggle someone in, he knew a way via a fire door and away from the cameras and, in any case, Harry wouldn't be too bothered if it was just a case of a bit of nooky on the side. Undesirables would get a different reception. They would be 'splattered'.

He walked the short way to the river. The night had grown a lot cooler, and the tide was coming in under a strange night sky—pale, almost white, like fog, so buildings and features such as walls and fences were indistinct and unreal. If you met another person, they loomed out of the mist like Magwitch in *Great Expectations*, giving you the fright of your life. Luckily, no one was around at this time. And there was a hint of salt and flower blossom on the breeze, which would normally have been pleasant and refreshing, but which seemed out of place in this mist. He longed for something more than a slight breeze; a cool wind would do.

He leaned on the rail and could just make out the surface of the water where the overhead lights lit it up. It bulged and heaved with incredible power. If you fell in there? No chance. At least the barrage should get to make plenty of energy.

So what had they had found in the two investigations? The link between Oliver Gladwyn and Johnny Puller looked interesting. And a disappearing girl. Secrets in the cupboard. Freddie the Ferret and his vendetta against the Gladwyns. Their tight organisation would take some bypassing. One for Mel with her Facebook tricks. It would have to be 'slowly, slowly catchee monkey' with Oliver Gladwyn, for Sarah Gladwyn had specified no approaches to her husband. And as for the terrorists, if the coppers and the NCA had found them difficult to crack, how could Jack and his outfit do any better?

Unless they got a stroke of luck, like with Roy's case. They could string it out for a bit for a few pay days, and then take the hit when Stuart got fed up with the lack of progress. No, the Gladwyn case looked like being the most productive.

The only problem with all of this was the feud between Roy and Mel. What could he do? He needed both of them. You could try and help Roy, but he was an alky with a death sentence. He wouldn't listen to reason. Why should he? Maybe Jack could support Mel with her childcare problems. But how? He had his own problems with a kid and uncooperative mother. He couldn't afford to pay for childcare for Mel. This psychopath of a partner could be tracked down and his legs broken. Or rather he could be warned off. Maybe if they hit the jackpot with both investigations and brought in more work, Jack could have a go at sorting it out. Trouble was, Roy was a bitter man, a misogynist; life hadn't turned out well for him. Easy to blame women. And Mel was feisty; she'd been fucked about by men and wasn't going to take any shit anymore.

He felt himself stiffening at the thought of Mel in her dressing gown with her eyes all sleepy and her blonde hair all tousled. No, that was one fantasy he could do without. The recurring dream he already had was bad enough. And, in any case, Mel had made her views clearly known—unless she was playing hard to get. Difficult to be sure. The one thing he didn't want was a kick in the goolies or a punch on the nose. Which with the present state of his hooter would be painful and messy.

He yawned. He felt really tired now. Maybe he could get some shuteye ...

*

The clinic was in one of those big Victorian houses that ringed Sefton Park, built with the cash from booming trade with the British empire, now slightly seedy, many converted to flats or hotels. No-one nowadays, apart from the very richest—and they wouldn't live in an area within walking distance of the scallies in Liverpool 8—could afford to keep an army of servants who, when the properties were built, were expected to live in the many small bedrooms. Some alternative medical practitioners, such as Jungian analysts, used a ground floor with its high, opulent plaster ceilings, heavy panelled doors and woodwork for consulting rooms—together with peaceful and secluded gardens. It provided a nice ambience for relaxing and talking things through. Standard counselling hadn't worked for Jack Gordon so someone in the personnel department had had the bright idea of sending him to a Jungian analyst.

It was a bit of a shock for Jack to find that Doctor A. Eastman was a woman. Adrianna. He had nothing against women, of course, but it had never occurred to him that he might talk about the very intimate things that had led him to this clinic in Sefton Park with one of them. She looked about ten years younger than Jack, and was very well manicured in a professional way: short dark hair, well-cut light-green suit. She made him feel at home straight away with a friendly greeting and ushered him from the reception into a room with a décor resembling one of those domestic interiors in a museum that show how people used to live in some past age—in this case the Victorian period.

The conversation started off a little stilted.

She explained Jungian therapy: 'It's a psychoanalytic approach that was developed by Carl Gustav Jung. He was a pioneer with Freud of modern depth psychology, particularly of the unconscious mind. Although Jung worked with Freud for some time, they eventually parted ways due to differing theories. Freud asserted that dreams and the unconscious are personal things contained within an individual, but Jung believed that the personal unconscious is only the top layer of a much deeper collective unconscious—the uncontrollable, inherited part of the human psyche which is made up of patterns—archetypes common to all humanity.'

Jack passed a hand over his head, pretending it was all beyond him. He had, of course, read up on the subject beforehand on Wikipedia, and many of the words and concepts were familiar to him.

She laughed. 'It's a lot to take in,' she said. 'The key thing is that in Jungian therapy these patterns can explain why we have habits we can't break, such as addictions, depressions and anxiety. It can help individuals see what's out of balance in their psyche and empower them to make changes that will help them to be more balanced and whole.' She paused, giving this a chance to sink in.

'So why have you come here for treatment, Jack,' she continued. 'Take your time. Jungian therapy is a talking therapy based on the counsellor treating the client as an equal.

My role is to help you find a way out of your problems. To be your friend.' She laughed and patted his hand. Her flesh felt cool.

Jack wondered if what he'd heard was true—that in Jungian therapy if your analyser was of the opposite sex you always fell in love with them. Though nowadays it would have to include members of the same sex.

'It won't all be sweetness and light, Jack. We will have to delve deep into your psyche, and what we come up with will sometimes be unpleasant. We call this revealing the Shadow. You may get irritated with me, even project your Shadow onto me, but believe me this is a process that must be gone through if you are to become balanced and whole.' She paused. 'Try telling me in your own words what your problem is. Take your time.' She reached down for a pad and pen. 'I'll take notes.'

'I was a policeman. Drugs squad. We did lots of undercover work. Liverpool was overflowing with drugs then. This innocent girl got murdered. She was a witness to a drugs-related murder and was reluctant to testify—the code in the rougher parts of Liverpool is not to be a grass—and I put pressure on her. Anyway, she disappeared, and her body was found in the river. It was supposed to be suicide, but I'm certain she was shoved in. It was covered up. The word in the canteen was that someone on the force was involved. I had no proof, so there was no way I could go around shouting about it. But I developed this feeling that I was somehow to blame. Got depressed, started drinking. Had a breakdown.'

'That must happen to many coppers, blaming themselves when things go wrong.'

'Yes, *but my dad was a copper. Beat bobby, then on the fraud squad. Took retirement just before I started, but he was a legend in the force. He implied that I was a wimp to get involved with "a little tart" as he called it. I needed to man up like a good copper.'*

'Problems living up to his expectations?'

'Exactly right.'

She made some notes. 'And your mother?'

He thought about this for a long time. Eventually he sighed. 'She left us when I was eight. Abandoned us really.'

'Why did she leave?'

'My dad was a bully. Not in any physical sense. But he used to do her down.'

She made some notes, then closed the pad. 'I think that'll be all for now. Mondays, Wednesdays and Fridays isn't it? See you same time Wednesday. This has been very interesting, Jack. There is one thing I would emphasise. I get this feeling that you are holding back. The essence of this therapy is to go for it. Reveal all. Don't hold anything back. Okay?'

CHAPTER NINE

Next day at the morning catch-up meeting everyone was bright-eyed and bushy-tailed. The air conditioning was working, and it was nice and cool. Lucy was looking after reception.

Jack poured himself a glass of water from the jug on the table. He was feeling better. His nose wasn't bleeding, and the aching had subsided, though a yellowish bruise was forming, only partially masked by the plaster. He'd dropped the cream suit off at the dry cleaners and put the washing on with the white shirt. Now he was dressed for action: grey sports jacket, dark blue open-necked shirt, blue jeans and brown brogues. Like one of those private eyes in the movies—Jack Nicholson, say, in *Chinatown* or Max Cherry in *Jackie Brown*. Max was a bail bondsman, of course, but to Jack he looked like an archetypal Hollywood private eye. And Faye Dunaway and Pam Grier—sexy little ladies. Yes, he did like private-eye movies from the seventies. Just so long as it wasn't present day stuff. They were never as good as the old ones. Especially remakes of the classics. God, he hated that.

'Mel. Take it away,' Jack said. 'What have you got?'

Mel read from her notes; her glasses perched on the end of her nose. 'All I can say is that it's an interesting family history. All the stuff about dead slate quarrymen and helping the English to steal Welsh water gives some valid reasons for the threats. But the family secrets are interesting too. Helen, the daughter, disappeared in 1983. Shortly afterwards the Gladwyns abandoned the house in Liverpool for the one in North Wales. And get this. Lord Gladwyn, Sarah's father, was involved in right-wing politics in the thirties. Knew Aleister Crowley.'

'The Beast?'

'Yeah, but there is evidence that that might have been character defamation by Welsh nationalists. All English lords at that time were suspected of being Nazi appeasers or devil worshippers or both.'

'This disappearance,' Jack said. 'What do the police records say?'

'Not much. There was a big search, but it's like she disappeared off the face of the earth after arriving at Lime Street Station to catch the train to North Wales.'

'Maybe she ran away with a lover. Any leads on that kind of thing?'

'Not a dicky bird.'

'There's the obvious one that she never boarded the train and was murdered.'

'It's likely. She was spotted getting out of a car in front of Lime Street station. Too fuzzy an image to identify the car, I'm afraid.' She paused. 'Then get this. Clothes found in a neat pile by the river at the Pierhead. Body never found. Recorded as suicide.'

There was a long pause as everyone took this in.

'Okay,' Jack said. 'We were employed by Mrs Gladwyn to investigate these threats from the anarchists and Freddie the Stoat—sorry, Ferret—not pry into family secrets. What about this Oliver character? He sounds dodgy. On the news every night spouting his trendy eco-warrior stuff.'

'Right,' Mel said. 'He's got some baggage: dropped out of university, became a traveller; arrested at Greenham Common, given a conditional discharge; teamed up with Johnny Puller—I'll come to him later.'

'Johnny Puller,' Roy said. 'I've heard that name somewhere.'

'Yup,' Mel said. 'Chief Exec of Mersey Estates. Anyway, the pair started off with cannabis smuggling and moved up the drugs supply chain until they were big players. The police had a big operation to nail the pair, but it went tits up when their main informant disappeared in Australia. And get this; he disappeared from a shark-infested beach. Clothes left

in a neat pile. I found an obscure newspaper article—
it's always worth checking the references at the end
of Wikipedia articles. The pair went off the police
radar for a few years —it's now a cold case—then
Oliver marries into the Gladwyn family and changes
his name.'

'Well done, Mel,' Jack said.

'Why all this focus on the Gladwyns?' Roy cut
in. 'Aren't they the victims? What about this Freddie
the Weasel character?'

'Freddie the Ferret,' Jack said. 'And it's
important to determine if what is being said about
the Gladwyn family had any basis in fact. Then we go
from there. Carry on, Mel.'

'The problem with Freddie and his anarchist-
class warriors is that they're mainly based in Bristol—
which is like the national capital of anarchism—with
outliers in big cities like Liverpool. It's a very tight
network: safe houses, computer encryption, the
works. The police can't get anywhere. They've tried
to infiltrate the organisation, but the agents are
quickly outed. I set up a fake Facebook profile for a
young lady with an interest in the environment—
against cutting down of ancient woodlands, fox
hunting, that kind of thing. Nothing so far. That sort
of thing takes time.'

'What I can't understand,' Roy said. 'Is why
these anarchists are so against this Mersey barrage.
I'd have thought it was just up their street. Clean,
carbon-free energy and all that.'

'It's complicated.' Mel laughed. 'They prefer solar and wind, and they say the barrage will cause environmental damage in the estuary. And they claim that it's just a cover for creating lucrative development sites. Which is where Mr Puller comes in. His company, Mersey Estates, is buying up land that will be opened up by the barrage development.'

'Mersey Estates?' Roy said. 'Are they the outfit with the purple signs that you see everywhere? It's like a disease.'

'They're the ones,' Mel said. 'The outfit has some dodgy stuff in its past—money laundering for organised crime. I'm chasing that at the moment.'

'Okay, Mel, good work,' Jack said. 'Stick at it. Roy?'

'Oh, what?' Roy was staring out of the window, lost in thought. 'Right. Aman Iman—water is life. The dossier from the NCA tells us that this is the latest ruse in the war between us and the Islamic terrorists. Security is so tight that they're trying to come from different directions. Instead of bombs, they want to put stuff in the water supply. But apparently, it's a difficult trick to pull off. You can put something like anthrax or even plague bacilli in a city's water supply, but it's difficult to ensure that it gets delivered to the end user efficiently. Bacteria and viruses often die when exposed to the elements, and they get flushed away.'

He paused.

'Of course,' he continued, 'the NCA have beefed up security at water supply points, reservoirs and the like. I've got a map of Liverpool here with them marked on. Not that many locations. And the terrorists are using Western-looking and sounding people. Although this group arose in the border areas of Libya and Tunisia in the Sahara Desert, they don't ride around on camels with towels on their heads.'

'Wasn't there a Jewish plot after the war to do something similar to German cities?' Jack said.

'The Nakam—revenge. That would be ironic wouldn't it? Islamists getting the idea from the Jews. I've put some background on that on the file. It was planned but never happened—the Jewish leaders were worried that it might hamper efforts to create a Jewish state. It probably wouldn't have worked anyway with the chemicals available then. You need something that's colourless, tasteless, disperses easily in water and doesn't get broken down. Arsenic is the obvious choice—though it's easily detectable these days.'

'And the police files?'

'Not much. It's difficult to infiltrate local Muslim communities as it is. They tend to be groups like the Somalis who keep themselves to themselves. And it's likely that the local communities wouldn't be involved anyway. There is one clue I found on the NCA files. They broke an encrypted email. Some stuff about a sleeper in Liverpool. Presumably not a rough sleeper, though I guess that's possible. Then the encryption was changed and there's been nothing since.'

'A sleeper,' Jack said. 'You mean someone local?'

'That's right. Someone with no obvious links to Islam or terrorism. Probably been lying low for years. Neither the plods nor the feds have anything further.'

'How are we supposed to follow that up?' Jack said. 'Wait for this character to get drunk in a pub and spill the beans? Not that a Muslim would go in a pub. No wonder they passed it on to us. A poisoned chalice or what?'

Roy shrugged. 'Don't ask me; I just work here.'

Jack's mobile rang. 'Excuse me for a moment.' He put the phone to his mouth. 'Yes?'

'It's Brian, Brian Hargreaves. Got a problem at the lodge. You've got to see it.'

CHAPTER TEN

Brian Hargreaves laughed and shook his shaven head—standard hairdo for builders these days. How did you get it that smooth and shiny, Jack wondered? Shave it every day, then give it a good polish?

'I'm not joking, Jack,' Hargreaves said. 'Come and see for yourself. But be careful to put your feet exactly where I put mine, and watch you don't walk into anything. You've done enough damage to your nose for one day.'

Ha, fucking ha, Jack thought. The latest plaster seemed to cover half his face as well as his nose. *I'm getting fed up with this. I feel like the Phantom of the fucking Opera.*

He followed Hargreaves up the stairs. They creaked with every footstep, and Hargreaves hugged the wall. Jack did as he had been told.

He'd bought the old lodge, built in the 1830s as an entrance lodge to Aigburth Hall, on a whim at an auction. The house—the original seat of the

Gladwyn family he'd recently discovered—had been demolished in the sixties and the site redeveloped in the seventies for posh detached houses. A high fence ruled out any interaction with the neighbours. Jack knew the listed building description by heart: sandstone, Doric porch and circular bay. Good price, except for all the work needed. The estimates had come in high, and he'd taken the lowest one, against his own better judgement.

Hargreaves stopped on the landing, and Jack joined him, standing as close as he could without invading the other man's personal space. What would his weight be? Jack guessed seventeen stones. That wouldn't help if the stairs and the floors were in danger of collapsing.

'The whole is place is riddled with it,' Hargreaves said. 'Come and look at this.' In the front bedroom several floorboards had been lifted, exposing the joists. Hargreaves knelt down and poked a screwdriver into a floorboard. 'See how spongy it is.' He put the screwdriver down and shone a torch into the hole. Jack knelt down to see. A mass of white and yellow fungus spread along the wood of the joist, like an alien in the fifties B-movie *The Blob* starring a young Steve McQueen. A huge globule of chewing gum spread through a cinema while teenagers screamed their heads off. Eventually it grew so big that it could engulf people, tubs of popcorn, cups of Coca-Cola and all.

'But why wasn't this identified at the start?' Jack said.

'It's a listed building,' he'd been told. 'Best get a proper architect to project manage it. You'll save in the long run.' But no, Jack had been worried about getting tracked down and had kept it all unofficial and gone for Hargreaves who worked cash in hand and had jobs on the go all over the place, most half-finished—he would disappear without warning, leaving rain pouring through the roof and down the walls.

And Jack had project managed the job himself. Got plans done by a cowboy from the *Echo*. Now Hargreaves was coming up with all sorts of extras that an architect would have picked up. Extras that Jack didn't have the money to pay for.

'It's wet rot, see,' Hargreaves said. 'Down to water getting in from the rusted rainwater gutters and pipes and seeping through the walls. Sandstone, see? Porous. Not obvious to the naked eye. It looks dry in this heat but wait till we get some rain. It only came to light when I put my foot through a rotten floorboard. All the affected wood will have to be cut out and replaced. And the sound wood treated. Joists, floors, windows, the lot.'

'And what will the damage be?' They were already wildly over budget, and he had run out of ready cash. He'd thought about going for a bank loan, but with his credit rating he'd have no chance.

'It'll have to be done by a specialist firm. Five thousand, maybe?'

'Five thousand? You're jokin' aren't yah? On top of the back wall?'

That made a total of ten thousand. Cash he didn't have. The bulge in the back wall meant it would have to be taken down and rebuilt. It was brick, unlike the front of the property, which was sandstone, but it'd still cost five thousand. A bulge like that would've been the first thing a professional architect would've picked up. He felt sick. His head was spinning.

'Give me some time to think about it, Brian,' he said eventually.

'Look, Jack. I hate to be the bearer of bad news, but that's what building jobs on old buildings are like. I had one of these down in Falkner Square. Total disaster. A previous builder went bust on account of it going way over budget. I picked it up for buttons, but it nearly did for me, too. We refurbished it for flats, but now it's a knocking shop.' He stopped and giggled at Jack's quizzical look. 'Go check for yourself if you don't believe me. It's the one in the middle on the south side. Directly opposite the entrance to the park.'

'A proper knocking shop? I thought they got rid of them ages ago along with the free parking on the street.'

'Oh, it's a step up from the old knocking shop with the red light in the window. Higher class. You can't tell from the outside. Advertised as a massage parlour. They closed down the old-style places with the method they used to get Al Capone: Taxes. The owners pay what's due or pay off the authorities. It's everywhere now; cops, council, politicians—they've all got their noses in the trough.'

Jack didn't respond. In Liverpool you often heard conspiracy theories involving the people in power.

'So an honest tradesman like myself gets nothing but grief,' Hargreaves continued. 'Look at all these restoration projects on the telly. Have you seen one that doesn't go over time and over budget? Where the rain's lashing down and the couple who started off with stars in their eyes are sitting with their heads in their hands? It's just one of those things, mate.'

Which was true. But a proper architect would have picked up on the bulge and the dry rot at the start. What a fool Jack had been.

On the way down the stairs, Jack didn't keep to the wall, and his foot went through one of the stair treads. Luckily, Brian grabbed his arm and stopped him going arse over tit down the stairs.

'See,' Brian said. He took Jack's arm and guided him down to the bottom. 'Rotten. That's what happens when the water gets in and you leave it for long enough.'

Hargreaves went to his van—an ex-post-office van, the red paint faded; you could just make out where the letters 'GPO' had been. He'd be off to the chip shop in Rose Lane that had a small café attached. Jack had seen him sitting in the window eating a big plate of fish and chips, drinking tea and reading a paper. He'd still been there when Jack had driven by half an hour later. It seemed to be his usual lunch and teatime venue when he worked at the lodge. Jack had wondered about it. Most builders were on the road by four—sometimes half three. Maybe Hargreaves lived by himself and didn't have much of a home to go to.

Jack's mobile rang again. He longed to turn it off, but it might be something important. He checked the caller. His dad. 'Jack?' he said. 'You promised to be early for once!'

Oh shit. His dad's birthday.

CHAPTER ELEVEN

Mel checked her watch: ten thirty. Mrs Morgan was due at twelve which didn't leave much time to keep the job rolling. Mel had set up the fake Facebook profile the day before and already many of the friend requests she'd sent out had received a positive response.

Some people were calling her by her first name already—Debbie, a nice common name, matched by a picture lifted from Google images. Pleasant but not too attractive. Even just a little untidy and plain. Really good-looking people with perfect styling tended to be distrusted on the net. It was like when you were buying a car, you went for the pleasant boy-next-door salesman rather than the flashy George Clooney type with the Hollywood smile.

The U.S. of A. had conveniently dropped out of the climate deal, and the internet was buzzing with condemnation. Mel had followed the arguments in

the papers and on the TV and could hold her own—
better if you weren't totally lying when you debated
an issue. 'If you can fake sincerity, the world's your
oyster' was a good line but, in her experience,
insincerity was magnified if you engaged in online
debates. And when it came to climate change, she
was all for action to stop it. What was the point of
bringing up a daughter if the world was going to hell
in a handcart?

It was interesting that no one was following
Trump's lead. Even the big republican states like
Texas were ignoring him and going for the cheaper
options of wind and solar. The thing was, coal
seemed on the way out no matter what anyone did.
And nuclear after Fukushima was too risky and
expensive. But best not to go overboard on
renewables just yet. Softly, softly, catchee monkey.

Personally, she couldn't see what all the fuss
was about if something was cheaper and cleaner than
the alternatives. What was there not to like? Unless
you worked for the oil, coal or nuclear industries and
your job was on the line.

As she posted and replied, she tried to
gradually edge the discussion round to the merits of
solar, wind (not barrages, just yet) and the iniquities
of nuclear and coal.

One respondent, Jane, picked up on this, and
they each made a series of long and emotional posts.
Jane took the trouble to make her posts well thought

out—she'd even checked her facts on Wikipedia a couple of times.

'So what do you think of the idea of barrages across estuaries?' Mel typed in. 'Use the sea. Carbon free energy so long as the tide keeps coming in and going out, as it has since the time of King Canute.'

'It's not as simple as that, Debbie,' came the response. 'The initial capital cost is so big—almost as much as nuclear—that the government has to get involved to underwrite loans from the big banks. Then it becomes part of the capitalist system. It's fine to use the sea so long as it doesn't harm the environment, which barrages do. Better to have offshore wind with benefit to local communities.'

Mel sat back and watched 'likes' with thumbs up symbols popping up. She wanted to respond along the lines of it being better to go for any form of renewable energy so long as it helped to save the planet but resisted the temptation. Instead she typed in:

'That's given me food for thought, Jane. I love your responses, so intelligent and well thought through. No knee jerks here!' Again, several likes, this time with heart symbols.

The phone rang to announce Mrs Morgan's arrival, Mel closed down the computer and sat back in her chair. A fruitful morning's work. She would leave the on-line debate for a bit. Don't look too keen. She remained motionless for a moment then stood up. Best get this over with.

She opened the door and gestured Brenda Morgan inside. For her, forty was a memory from long ago, though she was still trying to look thirty. From the wrinkles around her eyes and mouth and the obviously dyed mop of auburn hair, it looked like she would soon be contemplating that most dreadful of ages—fifty.

Once seated, Mel handed her the folder of photos. Brenda scanned the images, her jaw growing tighter as she leafed through them. When finished, she looked up. 'The bastard,' she said but with no emphasis or emotion. 'So is that it?'

'It's what you hired us for, Mrs Morgan.'

'I know,' Brenda said, 'but that'll mean more expense, won't it?'

Keep smiling sweetly.

'You took us on, Mrs Morgan, to get a result. Isn't that what you wanted?'

Brenda said nothing and stared over Mel's shoulder. She was obviously miserable about the results. Maybe she'd been hoping that they'd discover Mr Morgan to be innocent. Though that was unlikely given his past activities. He even looked like a sleaze-ball. Mel shuddered to herself. His hand would be clammy, like a wet fish. A greasy, dead fish. A violent wet fish. He'd head butted Jack Flash Gordon—cracked his nose open. She stifled a chuckle. She wished that she had a video of that—the look on his face.

Roy Hannon was a dickhead of the old school, but he was right about the violence when things got hot in this job. She always worked in pairs if she could. Safer. Or as safe as it could be in this sort of career. The women were the worst. They fought dirty, going for the eyes with their nails. Mel worked out and did karate when she could manage it. Luckily, she'd not suffered many attacks, but she shuddered at the thought of having to fend off someone like Morgan. It'd be like trying to defend yourself against one of those giant poisonous lizards; what did you call them, Komodo Dragons?

'Well,' Brenda said at last. She wrinkled her nose. 'What's that smell? Chips?

Mel didn't react.

'I suppose it's a good living if you don't think about it too much,' Mrs Morgan said.

Mel shrugged. 'Don't take it out on me, Mrs Morgan. It's an honest living. We provide a service for people who have a problem. Now, like I said, I suggest that you take these photos and show them to your solicitor.'

CHAPTER TWELVE

His dad's house was the only one of three remaining from a terrace, and the only one not boarded up. The group stood like an afterthought on the demolition site as if the JCB driver hadn't been able to finish the job on a Friday evening and had fucked off to the pub anyway.

One of Jack's tyres crunched a brick, so he parked up and walked the rest of the way.

He always found it strange to come back to his childhood home on the banks of the Mersey. As an only child, he roamed the narrow streets with the tightly packed houses and bits of woodland on the muddy banks of the river. Now the streets remained, with the odd brick or piece of debris, but most of the buildings had gone. You could even see the Clwyd hills in the distance on the other side of the river, which you never could before.

As usual, piles of the *Echo* in the hallway that almost reached to your waist cluttered the house—a terrible fire risk, but Gordon senior wouldn't listen. Jack's mother wouldn't have stood for it, but she'd left years ago. Jack hadn't seen her for years and didn't have her current address. He got an occasional Christmas card, and that was it.

His dad wouldn't listen to any criticism now. Jack suspected senility, but his dad wouldn't go to the doctors. And the musty smell—a mixture of old books and sweaty socks—was getting worse. Not as bad as Roy's place, but getting that way.

Today it was paranoia—his latest hobbyhorse.

'This fellow came to the door,' he said. They sat in the back room, facing each other. 'Showed me I.D., but I wasn't fooled. He was up to no good. Said he was from some company, Liverpool Estates—or something—buying up property. Well, I didn't fall for it, did I? The people on either side fell for that. Got buttons. Anyhow, a couple of days later the doorbell started ringing. Went to answer it, no-one there. Then dogshit through the letterbox, and the bins pushed over and emptied. I looked out the bedroom window and there were two fellers hanging about. Might have had *scallies* written on their backs in big letters.'

'Did you ring the police?'

'No point. They won't come down here.' He paused. 'What happened to your nose?'

'I walked into a door.'

'Nasty.'

'You should see the state of the door.'

Both pondered on this for a minute or so.

'Okay,' Jack said at last. 'Are you ready?'

Gordon senior had made an effort—washed, shaved, put on a suit and combed his hair. He had to be helped into the car, though.

'Look at all these fucking signs,' he said, pointing as they drove along. 'Now that's where that lad said he was from, Mersey Estates not Liverpool Estates.'

It was true. Virtually every house had a black and purple *For Sale* sign with the Mersey Estates logo. Seemed to be taking over Liverpool. Jack worried about his dad's swearing. At one time he'd been so strict about it; no swearing in the house. He'd even caned Jack when he was an eleven-year-old kid for swearing.

His dad liked the pub by the river. Jack would've preferred somewhere a bit better, but he went along with the old man—he was the birthday boy. And the pub had air conditioning, so at least it was cool, almost cold enough to start shivering.

'What do you think of this Trump?' Gordon senior said once they were seated at a table in a window.

'I dunno,' Jack said, hiding his true feelings. 'Maybe his bark is worse than his bite.

'Well, I like the cut of his jib! We need someone like him to sort out this Brexit malarkey. What we want is our country back, not pay the krauts in sausages only to get our frigging bananas all bent to fuck.'

An elderly gent sitting by himself at a nearby table and reading the newspaper with a bottle of white wine, looked up, adjusted his glasses and stared at Gordon senior—who didn't say anything more on this subject. Jack breathed a sigh of relief. At one time his dad had been a big union man, and thoughtful with it. Now he blurted out anything that came into his head, mixed with swear words. The more people around to hear the better. Alzheimer's? Tourette's? Dementia? His dad would never go in for a check-up.

'I've been watching this programme on Channel Five,' his dad said. 'It's all about how things like 9/11 were faked. Did you know that the moon landing was faked?'

'Really?' Where had this come from?

'Yeah it was all set up in a Hollywood studio. All the German scientists went home you see, and they were stuck. So they faked it.' Pause. 'You know that Hess was as mad as a fucking hatter?'

The swear words were starting again. Soon it would be embarrassing. His dad had guarded Rudolph Hess and Albert Speer at Spandau prison during national service, and he loved to tell tales from the time.

'Nasty piece of work. Used to throw cigarettes to sentries, and if they accepted them he'd report them and get them into trouble. Used to sit on this seat and bend over and throw his arms in the air ...' his dad threw his own arms in the air, 'and go, "Uhh-Uhh-Uuh!"'

The elderly gent carefully folded his newspaper and went into the bar with his bottle of wine. Jack looked around. No-one within earshot. The last time he'd taken his dad out a man with a family had collared Jack on the way to the loo and asked him to 'ease off on the bad language'.

Then Jack remembered. Reminiscence therapy. 'Ah, Dad,' he said. 'Policing's not like it used to be.'

'Thieving was a lot simpler in the old days, Jimmy lad.' Gordon Senior already had the faraway look in his eyes. 'They robbed post offices, hijacked lorry loads of spirits off the docks, a bit of safe-cracking. The thieves were good, honest people, none of this drugs malarkey. They were great days them, chasing after villains—best days of me life. They had skills, you know. Cracking a safe isn't easy. You need to know about combinations, metals, alloys, chemistry. It was a science. Now it's just beating people up or shooting them. Stitching a bloke's face onto a football.' He stopped and looked at Jimmy. 'Don't laugh. It really happened. Wacker Hughes. Nice bit of stitching too.'

'I remember that. Bad do. Sorry, you were telling me about the old days, Dad.'

'It all kicked off in the war, see. I was born in 1938 and I can remember the sound of those Fokkers overhead: Wuh ... whuh. Wuh ... whuh. There were loads of bombed-out buildings, blackouts, the scuffers over-stretched. Yanks with ciggies, nylons, wads of cash. And the girls used to wear American knickers—one Yank and they're down. The lads used to get girls to lure the Yanks into dark alleys then cosh them and rob their stuff. And the docks were packed with gear. Ciggies, whisky, you name it. There were all these gangs. The Peanut gang—they used to split open sacks of peanuts on the docks and hand them out to the kids. The Little Gangsters—they'd break into cars and go joyriding. Bomber Command—they used to drop bricks on cars from pedestrian bridges. Just for the fun of it. The Forty Thieves—they'd pack into a shop, all forty of them, and rob all the stuff. Then it was the Teddy Boys. I was one, you know, before I joined the force. I had this fantastic tailor-made suit with velvet lapels. Me ma had a few bob then and she paid for it. Proper gear it was. And big beetle-crusher shoes. We used to hang out in the dance halls and at the fairs. It was just fighting at first, before the robbing.'

'Did you ever come across a guy called Johnny Puller when you were on the fraud squad, Dad?'

'Did I? Biggest rogue in Liverpool. Got others to do the dirty work. Started off as a traveller, then got into pushing drugs and finally organised crime. He got in at the right time, too. Chuckie, the top man was in jail and his sidekick, Wacker Hughes, had to take over. He met a sticky end, and his nephew Jimmy had to take over in his turn. Jimmy's heart wasn't in it and he got out—retired to the sun—and passed it all over to Puller.'

'So how did the fraud work, then?' This was good. His dad was back in the past. He got out his little notebook and a pen. Gordon senior didn't notice.

'We used to call it "Money Laundering for Pleasure and Profit". And they were very good at it— we never managed to nail them. See, Jack, the big problem with most criminal activity is that it's cash rich. But there's only so much you can do with cash. Nowadays you can't buy a house or a car with readies. You need to launder it. So what they did was set up a construction company and a security company. You pay cash-in-hand employees in addition to legit ones to bid low for contracts and win them. Another way is to buy up a failing company, in double glazing, say—that's a common one—and pay cash bonuses to legit staff. That gives you an edge over your competitors. You get lots of favourable reviews on your web-site and you're raking in the work and the cash.'

He paused, took a sip of his beer, and then he was off again. 'Anyway, they set up Sefton Park Security and Cherry Tree Construction.'

'Sefton Park Security; wasn't that run by that mad bastard, Jamaica Jim, the feller who killed his wife with a machete?'

'Yeah. Nice guy, Jim. Very polite, a gentleman. Anyhow, profits from the two operations were fed into a property company, to buy—you guessed it—property. Now everything is legit—taxes, NI and all that, paid and on time so you don't attract attention. Trouble is, you needed to be an accountant rather than an old-style copper to sort out something like that and nail the twats.'

He finished his pint.

'So that's where Mersey Estates came from,' he continued. 'Once the cash is gone you can't prove anything. No documentary evidence. And no-one's going to snitch, either—too scared. And if you were protected by corrupt coppers and politicians, Bob's your uncle. Perfect money laundering scenario. Just got to make sure everyone gets paid on time.' His eyes were shining. 'I kept out of it, of course, but they were happy days, Jack.'

Hey Jude began to play in the background, presumably on a piped music loop. Gordon senior listened with great attention until the chorus started, then he sang along loudly.

'You know Paul McCartney was murdered in 1966 by Brian Epstein?' he said.

'What?'

'Yep, it was a Jewish conspiracy. His body was fed to pigs on a farm in Gloucestershire. The feller who claims to be him is a look-alike. It was all explained on this programme on BBC Five, presented by that David Ikea feller. Now he knows what he's talking about. What are you laughing at?'

'Yeah, and Stalin was an American spy. I bet that was on the telly, too.'

'Oh ye of little faith. That was Harold Wilson, silly boy. He was a Soviet spy.' Gordon senior spoke as if explaining something obvious to a small child. 'I don't know why you act like you do, Jack. Getting up on your high horse and calling these scientifically proven things conspiracy theories. I suppose you still deny the existence of a conspiracy in the Liverpool establishment.' He laughed. 'You could have been part of the project to dig up the evidence, but instead you took the easy way out—on a sick note.'

'What!' Jack was angry now. He'd had enough of these conspiracy theories. His dad had never been like this before he became unwell. He'd fallen for all this conspiracy stuff hook, line and lead weights. It was a classic way of making sense of a confusing world: secret knowledge and psychological projection. He'd googled it. But this reference to his early retirement was poisonous. He tried to hide his anger, but it was difficult.

The food arrived. Jack picked at his chicken while his dad piled into a plate of fish and chips. The menu had listed: *beef, lamb, chicken and pork*, and at the bottom *vegetarian option—just have the roast potatoes and vegetables*.

'Excuse me,' Gordon senior said, grabbing the arm of a waiter who was scurrying past carrying two plates piled high with Sunday roast. He nearly caused the lot to be deposited into Jack's lap.

'Yes, sir,' the waiter, a lad who looked about fourteen, said.

'This fish has bones in it.'

The lad looked amazed. 'It's fish, sir. Fish have bones.'

'Well, I don't like bones. They stick in your throat. Health and safety. Ever heard of it? Kindly fetch the manager.'

The lad nodded, delivered the plates to a family sitting at a table in the corner and, eyes fixed forward, disappeared into the back room.

An explosion of laughing and swearing sounded in the bar—Jack distinctly heard the c-word—then a big fellow staggered into the room, obviously well-plastered. He walked through to the toilets with a big grin on his face, happy about something. Jack wondered how the man with the newspaper and the bottle of wine was finding it.

'That's one of them,' Gordon Senior said. 'The ones who've been harassing me. That's Gobby Gilbertson. His mate's Eddie Malone, Mick's brother. Gobby's a two-hundred-and-fifty-pound gorilla with a brain to match, but Eddie's a nasty, sly piece of work.'

CHAPTER THIRTEEN

'Okay, okay, Mr P, we're working on it.' The man listened as whoever was on the other end of the line spoke. The tone got harsher—Jack could hear it from several yards away where he stood just inside the entrance to the pub—and the man's face folded into a grimace.

'Don't worry, Mr P, we're working on the hold-out. He'll be gone before you can say Jurgen Klopp.'

'Mr P' must be Johnny Puller. The harsh tones came again.

'Right, right,' the man said. He switched off the mobile. 'Knobhead.'

Jack had worked his way as close as he dared on the other side of a partition. Now he edged slowly back.

'Eddie?' came a shout from the bar. 'Another pint?'

'What do you think, Gobby? I always want another pint. Knobhead!'

The man who'd been speaking into the mobile must be Eddie Malone. And his honey monster mate would be Gobby Gilberston. A new waiter, looking about the same age as the previous one and in the uniform white shirt and black trousers, came by. Jack turned and headed for the toilet.

'Do you want to order food?' the kid said.

'No, we've had our lunch.' Jack smiled.

'Would you like a dessert, sir?' the kid said brightly, no doubt following his training.

'What a good idea,' Jack said. 'Take the menu to that old chap sitting over there,' Jack pointed at the old gent with his newspaper and bottle of wine, 'and get him whatever he wants. Add it to our bill— Gordon, table six.'

The kid nodded and swept away.

Malone's head appeared around the partition. Then Gobby's appeared next to Malone's like a vaudeville act. Malone's head was small with a pointed snout and little beady eyes like a ferret's, and Gobby's was big, like a fridge.

'Where you listening in on me, nosy?' the small head asked. The big head laughed at the witticism. 'That was a private conversation, knobhead,' the small head said. 'Are you with that old get over there, the one who lives down by the river? Perhaps my mate can escort you round the back and we can have a quiet conversation about this.'

Jack strode through the open doors at the back of the pub and into the car park. The two followed him and, when Jack broke into a trot, so did they. He ran up a slope, the grass dried out and slippery. After a few strides sweat ran into his eyes; he wiped them with the back of his hand and hopped over a low wooden fence and into woodland. He ran down a path for maybe a hundred yards, then stopped to catch his breath at a black-and-red, Chinese-style pagoda in front of a small lake with reed beds around the sides. The water had receded until there was only a small pool choked with lily pads, surrounded by a wide expanse of dried out, cracked mud.

Jack must've lost them. He looked around. *This must be the Festival Gardens.* Disused since 1984 though someone was obviously maintaining the site as the grass was neatly cut and the footpaths were free of litter. He stepped onto a wooden boardwalk below a small cliff created by piling up sandstone blocks.

'Oi!' came a shout. 'We only want to talk to you, knobhead!'

Oh yeah? They wanted to do more than 'talk'. Jack ran up a long set of wide steps and was breathing hard when he got to the top. Then more woodland. He stopped at the edge of the trees. An overgrown car park—a big expanse of concrete studded with piles of bricks and rubbish—stretched towards Otterspool Park and, beyond, an industrial area with factory units visible over a dilapidated concrete-panel fence. A bird sang somewhere.

He could see the walkway along the Mersey—a wide path with grass on one side and the river on the other with metal railings to stop anyone falling in. No good. Once out there, you'd be visible for hundreds of yards. And he didn't like being down by the water's edge. Once, when he was a kid, he'd got stuck in the mud and only just managed to get out before the Mersey Bore—a five-foot-high wave of seething brown water—swept by.

He recognised the area from a map he'd seen recently in the paper. This was where the barrage would go from. The garden festival site, the industrial area beyond and then the land containing his dad's house beyond that made up the wider site that would be made developable by the barrage. He crouched down by a large tree and listened. Nothing. He moved into a sitting position with his back to the tree. Almost invisible now, he could relax. From his place on top of a small grassed bank, he could easily see anyone coming.

The Wirral sat on the other side of the Mersey—woods, low industrial buildings, a church spire—and beyond, the undulating grey line of the Welsh hills. He craned his neck around the tree. Off to the left he could see the chimneys of chemical works, wind turbines like a scene for *The War of the Worlds*, with the backdrop of the Helsby and Frodsham hills. Quite a panorama. Breathing quietly now, he listened. Just birds singing, a gull down by the river. A wood pigeon started up its five-note call, 'Uh huh huh, uh huh,' like Barry White serenading a sexy little lady friend.

A car engine barked nearby. It sounded like the exhaust was totally shot. Jack looked through the trees just in time to see a car flash by. He crept forward to the edge of the overgrown car park. A car roared around the big expanse of concrete, doing handbrake turns, the engine barking loudly. A new Ford Escort. Stolen? Two kids in the front seats. The car stopped, reversed, then sped off out the car park entrance.

He saw something moving a few yards away and went over. Some sort of animal making little gasping noises. Prickly. A hedgehog. Not rolled up. It looked surprisingly thin, like a rat with a spiky overcoat glued to its back. Little black, beady eyes with a pink snout, blood bubbling as it tried to breathe. The idiots in the car must have run it over. It was obviously in pain and a goner but what could he do? Kill it with a brick? No, he couldn't do that.

He stood for a long time, pondering what to do. Then he snapped to attention. His dad was alone in that pub. And those two jokers might've gone back to harass him. He'd have to move.

His mobile beeped. Mel.

'Hi, Jack. Good news. I've got an address.'

CHAPTER FOURTEEN

'Sort of a let me cry on your shoulder and you can cry on mine kind of thing?' Mel said. 'Best put on something quieter. We are on surveillance after all.'

Jack had been drumming his fingers on the steering wheel to *Rain* by The Cult.

Mel didn't look her best—dry hair, bags under her eyes. Jack probably looked much the same, so he couldn't talk. The van was still in for repairs, so they were in Jack's car. If one of them were to be caught short, there was no access to the back and a convenient urine ziplock bag, male or female version.

'Yeah. That kind of thing,' he said. He'd been thinking about the dream. Lack of sleep was beginning to tell. He needed to talk to someone. Anyone. 'You can kick off.' He fast forwarded the track to a new one and turned the sound down a bit.

'Everything but the Girl!' Mel exclaimed. 'I love them!' She glanced at him. 'How do I know you'll keep your bargain?' She paused before continuing, 'Oh well, you know most of this. I had a property firm in Solihull. Well, more like a house renovation company. Then I discovered that my husband had been stealing from the accounts ...'

'House renovation. Did you do up any old houses?'

'A few. Stop butting in. It's hard enough as it is.'

'Sorry, it's just that I'm having problems with the lodge.'

'That white elephant.'

'Well, I'm stuck with it now. Sorry; go on.'

'Not much to tell. Company went bust. Got divorced. Single parent.' She paused, obviously finding this hard. 'It's funny really. When I met Ged Gibson, I thought it was the best thing that had ever happened to me. He was so tall and handsome. Always smiling. I know it sounds like a cliché, but it's true; he was like a movie star, every woman's dream. But when I got pregnant it all went tits up. So to speak. Everyone knows that things change for a couple when a kid comes along—sex, sharing chores, cleaning up poo and vomit. You've just got to man up—well, woman up—and work together as a team until you get through it. But no, Gerard David Gibson was like a spoilt child; still a mother's boy, expecting me to do everything. And I could never get it right. He started to accuse me of not showing him enough affection and attention. '

She took a deep breath. 'Sorry but I need to get this off my chest, Jack,' she said. 'Then one day, just before I was due, as I came in the house, he rushed at me and punched me right between the eyes. He dragged me into the kitchen, with me trying to protect the baby in my stomach and my head from the blows. Then later he came over and was super loving, saying he'd lost control and I needed to be more aware of his moods so I wouldn't make him feel bad again.'

She stopped talking and wiped her eyes with a tissue. 'Later,' she continued, 'I researched it—it's classic psychopathic behaviour, blaming the victim. When the time came for the birth, he refused to attend. I became very stressed and had a difficult delivery. When I got home, he was brooding and angry. Then I lost it and screamed at him to pull his weight—that it was his baby too. He attacked me—punched me to the ground. It was incredibly painful so soon after I'd given birth. I fled to a friend's house with the baby. She took us to the hospital but, apart from some bruising, there was no direct evidence of an assault for the police to do anything. Or so they said. Useless bastards. I returned to him and he beat me up again. He told me he owned me, and if I tried to leave again, he'd kill us both.'

'It sounds like he needed to be taught some manners,' Jack said. 'If that happened to a relative of mine, we'd have got together a posse of vigilantes and broken his legs.'

'Yeah, well I didn't have family nearby. I was on my own. Anyway, I tried to leave—went to a refuge. But he tracked me down and kept following me. The supermarket, the petrol station; he'd be there making little signs mimicking a knife cutting a throat. Then I heard he'd been arrested for killing a complete stranger for no reason. He was put behind bars, but I worry that they'll listen to his smooth talk and release him. He's probably out by now. He's clever, a good talker. He'll claim that he's changed but he never will; it's his nature.'

She paused and laughed—a forced laugh. 'My dad and brothers bullied me, too.'

'I thought you were supposed to look after your kid sister?'

'In a normal family. And I was a right oddball at school, a misfit. Bullied, just like what's happening to my daughter now. Can't trust men. Don't laugh. Most are bullies or depressives. Same thing usually. Present company excluded.' She blew her nose into a tissue. 'To get to the meat of it,' she continued after a moment, 'there I was with a kid and no job. Until you came along, Jack. For which I'm eternally grateful.' She laughed. 'Not that grateful. Now it's your turn. You were a copper, weren't you?'

'Sure was. Detective sergeant. Drugs squad. Good at the job. Then we had this case involving this pimp who had a drug-dealing side-line. Right nasty piece of work. He got the idea that one of his girls was a grass. Really sad case this girl. Abuse at home, dysfunctional family, the lot—'

'Dysfunctional? That's a bit of a long word for a copper.'

'Things are changing. Not all coppers are thick plods. Nowadays they have degrees. They know about sociology, psychology. I've got a degree, you know. I was at Bristol University. I'm not just a thick ex-copper who becomes a glorified security guard.'

'You should have heard what Mrs Morgan had to say about our little enterprise.'

'What? That we're just cheap snoopers?'

'Got it in one.'

'I hope you told her that we provide a service for people like her.'

'Sure did.'

'Anyway,' he said, 'this innocent girl got murdered—she was a witness to a drugs-related murder and was supposed to have jumped in the river, but I'm certain she was pushed. And it was covered up. Someone in the force. I've got an idea who it was, but I've got no proof so I can't go around shouting about it. And, although it wasn't my fault, I got the idea that I was somehow to blame. Had a breakdown. Had therapy.'

'Therapy?'

'Yeah. Jungian psychiatrist, the works. The things I could tell you about my animus, my persona and my shadow...'

Mel passed a hand palm down over her head and made a blowing sound with her lips. 'Animus? Isn't that intense hatred?'

'Well, yes. But it's also a Jungian term for the male archetype.'

'Very appropriate.'

'No, there's a lot in it. It worked for me. Even got the dream under control.'

'Dream?'

'Yeah, I used to get this nightmare. And recently it's come back. Years after the analysis. That's the reason I'm so shagged out. And I need to talk about it.'

'Well go on, tell me about the dream.'

'I'm floating in the air over a city at night. It's drizzling lightly; I can feel it on my face.'

'In a dream?'

'Yeah; it's a realistic dream—full sense impressions and sound effects. I gradually sweep down until I'm above a square with a park in the middle, dimly illuminated by streetlights. There's a small lake in the park at one end of the square. On it is a small island with a single tree illuminated by a shaft of sunlight—'

'I thought you said it was night-time?'

'It is. But this is a dream with its own logic. Anyway, my attention is caught by something. On the grass in the middle of a square behind railings, a group of figures are gathered around something. They're all wearing greyish-yellow raincoats glistening with dampness from the rain. I land and creep forward. They're roasting a person on a spit over a fire.'

'Gross!'

'Yeah. The person is tied to a metal rod and is screaming and trying to break free. I can smell the roasting flesh and hear the screams. Like I said, full sound effects and sense impressions. One of the figures turns. I see his face clearly. He licks a spot of grease from his upper lip and screws up his face with pleasure. Then I wake up.'

'Wow,' Mel said. 'So was the person being tortured the girl?'

'It wasn't clear. The therapist explained it all.' He grinned. 'The tortured person came from my feelings of depression and guilt. But the tree in the shaft of light was a goal, something to aim at in life. I went through the whole process with her. Felt better, and the dreams stopped. But I had to resign from the police. Couldn't face it. I couldn't go back, and I couldn't get a normal job, so I set up this little operation. Everything was going fine until about two weeks ago when I started to get the dream again.'

'Do you know why?'

He shrugged. 'No idea.' He stared ahead. 'It gets worse. I can't have sex ...'

She laughed.

'Don't laugh; it's true,' he said. 'There's no point in dating or looking for a new partner. Whenever I get to the point when we're doing it, I get this idea that the woman I'm with is this girl. I can even see her face. I can't do it. And then it looks like I'm impotent.' He didn't add that nature will always find a way out. His frustration would build up until he had a wet dream in his sleep accompanied by a stomach-twisting nightmare.

'But you've got this reputation for being a lad. And you were married, weren't you?'

He stared into nothing for a while, then continued. 'Someone once said that you can never find happiness with another person. They always run off and leave you or they die. I was married. It wasn't perfect, but it was good while it lasted. Now she won't allow access yet she's happy to take the money every month.' He laughed. 'Start the violin machines.' He lapsed into silence again.

'Shit,' she said after a while.

'Look, Mel,' he said, not looking at her. 'I know you and Roy don't get on—'

She thumped her fist into the dashboard. 'Don't get on! I've had enough of being bullied in my life. I'm just not having it, Jack. The worst thing is, he's a wreck. If I hit him on the head, I'd break his legs. How would that suit you?'

Jack laughed. 'It's not him talking, Mel. It's the alcoholism. His kidneys are fucked. He's being poisoned by them.'

'Yeh? Well he belongs in a hospital then.'

Another long silence.

'Look,' he said. 'I'll try and get him sorted. You work with me or from home. Don't go near him. He can work on the water terrorism job. He likes going around pubs and listening in to conversations; that's how he cracked that drugs gang. We can work on Freddie and the Gladwyns. We make a good team, don't we?'

She thought about this for a moment, then slapped his thigh. 'Anyway! I like you, Jack.'

'What, now you know I'm impotent?'

'No, but in the right circumstances it might have happened between us.'

'Isn't it pretty to think so?' Jack said.

Mel looked away then turned at a sudden movement off to one side. 'Shit,' she said. 'That was quick.' She started the engine, but the other car shot by, going the opposite way. She started to turn their car but stopped. 'He's gone. We must have been spotted.'

*

'So tell me about your childhood.' Dr Eastman looked very professional today in black polo-necked jumper and slacks, and a small silver brooch and earrings. 'Any brothers or sisters?'

'None. I was an only child. We had a house with a big garden, down by the river. I spent a lot of time by myself— a solitary child. My dad was always at work, sometimes till late at night. My mother had her friends. Never at home.'

'Did anything happen that you feel bad about? Ashamed? Don't worry about it getting outside this room. As your therapist I'm held to secrecy. Like a priest at confession. Did you ever shoplift, for instance? Do something a policeman's son shouldn't do?'

He thought long and hard. 'There was the time I twisted my pet rabbit's ear.' He winced. 'I was about six. I know it sounds terrible. I've never told anyone. I did it just to see what would happen. It screamed and went limp.'

'Was it hurt?'

'No. It jumped up, right as rain. I got all sorts of treats for it to make up—carrots, lettuce and suchlike. But the next week at school, I found this beautiful peacock butterfly and walked round with it on my wrist, showing it to everyone. Well, this kid reached over and scrunched it up, killed it. I attacked this kid and tried to claw his eyes out. Got into all sorts of trouble, but it was worth it.

'I would've done the same. Hardly something to feel guilty about; not like some really bad act carried out by your shadow.'

'My shadow? What's that when it's at home?'

'It's the archetype that reflects deeper, darker elements of our psyche—our repressed ideas, instincts, weaknesses, shortcomings and desires.'

'What, like Dr Jekyll and Mr Hyde? There was a cruel little bastard inside of me?'

She laughed. 'If you like. The problem is when people project their shadow onto others. In Jungian analysis, the individual is encouraged to integrate their shadow and their real self. Self-acceptance is the key to wholeness. Anything else?'

He took a long time to reply. 'I was assaulted,' he blurted out, against his will.

'Sexually?'

He nodded. 'I was about eleven. Last year of junior school. I went scrumping for apples in a neighbour's garden. A man—a teenager, really—caught me. He took me into a shed, tied my hands behind my back and blindfolded me. I could feel something going on, then something wet and warm on my hand. I shook the blindfold off and looked down. His penis was over my hand, all purple and swollen, almost glowing, and my hand was covered in white stuff. I later realised it was sperm. I hadn't reached puberty, and there was no internet stuffed full of porn films then, so I didn't know what it was. And ...'

'Go on.'

'I started to get this recurring dream ...'

'Ah, dreams. I was going to get onto them. But ... go on.'

'I'm flying through the air, effortlessly, like some big-winged bird that flies across oceans—an albatross, say. I come to a castle sitting at the edge of a loch. It's quite wild—the Highlands of Scotland, maybe.' He stopped. 'I suppose flying is about sex, isn't it? I've read Freud. I was nearing puberty.'

She laughed. 'This is Jungian therapy, not Freudian, but, yes, flying is usually about sex.'

'I land close to the castle and go in. It seems there's treasure there. I walk up stone stairs, expecting to find a beautiful young girl with long golden hair, like in the fairy tale, sitting on a treasure chest. But when I get there it's dark with

*only slits in the walls for light. The floor is bare and dusty, and
a horrible monster's lying in the middle of the room—about
fifteen-foot-long, hairless, no limbs, like a giant maggot ...'*

'Or a giant penis.' She laughed.

*'Exactly.' He laughed, too. 'Even I can see the
symbolism of that after the assault.'*

'And then what happens?'

*'It's strange. You'd expect a fifteen-foot monster to be
a fearful, dangerous thing, what with its mouth stuffed with
sharp teeth, but I feel sorry for it, stranded in some dusty castle
away from its home in the sea. I find a rope, put it around it
and drag it down the steps to the loch. It's hard, but I manage
it. I pull it into the water and release the rope. It swims strongly
away, rising from the water for a moment, then coiling down
into the deep, like the Loch Ness monster or something from
Moby-Dick.'*

*She made some notes. 'The sea, of course, is the
commonest symbol for the unconscious,' she said. 'And it's
interesting that you didn't feel threatened by this monster.' She
made another note. 'And what about school?'*

*He shrugged. 'Not much to tell. I was Billy-No-
Mates. No one dared to actually bully me. I was quite a big
lad for my age, but I was considered a bit of a weirdo. One lad
did try it, but when I told my dad, he lost his temper, dragged
me round to this kid's house, and when he came to the door,
my dad thrust me at this kid so our heads collided and he was
temporarily knocked out. My dad being a copper meant that
he got out of it, but afterwards I was left alone.' He sighed.
'And then my mother left.'*

She made some notes. 'Right, Jack. That's enough for today. I'll see you on Friday.'

CHAPTER FIFTEEN

Roy looked worse than usual at the morning catch-up meeting: grey and unshaven; hair uncombed; staring out of the window. Probably been on a bender the night before. Everyone avoided direct eye contact. Mel, aware that the team had messed up, read a page in a file open in front of her with great concentration. Lucy gazed at the wall. Jack shuffled papers

It was too early in the day for the fryer to be operating in the chippy next door, and too early for the heavy metal fans from the flat on the other side. The air conditioning whirred away, keeping the room reasonably cool. Outside was as hot as ever even though the sun was a washed-out disc in an overcast sky. Could it be the start of a change? Maybe rain?

'So the trail's run cold,' Jack said. The aching in his nose had stopped, and he'd removed the plaster. He had a big bruise and three narrow strips of transparent adhesive on his nose, but at least he didn't look like an extra from *Casualty*.

'I thought you had him cornered,' Roy mumbled. 'This Freddie the Weasel.'

'Freddie the Ferret.'

'So what happened?'

Jack felt reluctant to talk about it. He was supposed to be a professional private investigator. First, he'd allowed himself to be head-butted by the subject of an investigation—what kind of a green recruit trick was that to pull? And now he'd been let down by slipshod surveillance.

'He slipped away,' he said. 'He's had a lot of practice. The cops and the authorities have trouble keeping tabs on him.'

'Probably got away on account of you two playing lovey-dovey as usual. Though personally I wouldn't bother. The Australian ham actor's better looking.'

Silence descended for several seconds as everyone took this in. Mel gathered her papers together, scraped back her chair and stalked out, slamming the door behind her. Jack and Lucy both jumped up and followed her into the corridor, but she was down the stairs and out the front door before they could stop her.

When they got back to the room, Roy was muttering to himself. Jack caught the words 'knickers' and 'Lady Muck'. He motioned to Lucy.

She followed him into the small tea-room, closing the door to the conference room behind them.

'What are we going to do with him, Lucy?'

She shook her head. 'He's getting worse. Is it Tourette's?'

'I dunno. He won't go to the doctors. He only gets treatment when he collapses in the street and has to be taken in an ambulance to hospital. I'm not a doctor or a psychiatrist. I've read up on it, but there's nothing I can do if he won't co-operate. Trouble is, he's effective—like in that Malone drugs case.'

'Isn't that what your dad's got?'

'They considered it as a possibility, but it seems that it's just plain old Alzheimer's with him. His embarrassing outbursts aren't too different to Roy's, but it's more him being a crusty old get than Tourette's, though he won't go to see the doctor either.'

'Sorry to sound so ignorant but what's the difference between Alzheimer's and Tourette's?'

'I'm not exactly an expert myself, Lucy. I've googled it and printed off the articles—a doctor in the know would say a little knowledge is dangerous. But, basically, Tourette's is a motor tic. It's not degenerative or life-threatening like Alzheimer's, and it's not usually associated with the blurting out of swear words like you see in the films. Medication's available, but there's nothing I can do if he won't go and see a doctor. It might just be that he is a crusty old sod and his screwed-up liver is making him more irritable.'

'And Alzheimer's?'

'That's different. It's a chronic neurodegenerative disease that gets worse over time—short term memory loss, apathy, confusion, depression. Depression for everyone involved, actually. He's had the diagnosis, and I'm trying to handle it.'

'No family to help?'

'My mother left us years ago. I'm an only child.

'It must be hard.'

'Yes.'

Neither spoke for a few moments.

'I don't know how long Mel is going to put up with it,' Lucy said at last. 'We need her.'

'We need him, too. He's a pain in the butt, but he's got a habit of coming up with the goods. Though I'm seriously contemplating putting him put out to grass. This accreditation business could be the excuse I'm looking for. Best if I go back in and try and talk to him. Try and keep things going for the time being.'

'Just keep the two of them apart,' Lucy said. 'You go in, I'll follow in a while.'

Back in the conference room, Roy was sitting by himself, muttering and staring down at the table. 'I'm sorry, Jack,' he said, not looking up. 'It's not me;

it's my liver. It's spreading poison into my body. I can't stop myself.'

'Roy, we can't go on like this. You've upset Mel. That was totally uncalled for. In most workplaces you'd have been sacked on the spot.'

Roy stared at the table.

'Look,' Jack said. 'Have a few days off. Take your laptop and mobile and do a bit of work from home. I'll keep in touch. Try and get some leads on this water terrorism malarkey. I'll give you a lift home. And will you try and cut down on the pop?'

The trouble was, Roy did his best work in pubs, so it wasn't exactly logical to ask him to cut down on his drinking. But there was a happy medium.

Roy lifted his head and looked Jack right in the eyes. 'I'll give it a real go this time, Jack.'

Jack waited while Roy went to get the laptop. He sat down in a chair with a thump. They'd reached a dead end. Freddie had escaped after sterling work by Mel, but now he knew they were on his tail, and he'd probably recognise Jack and Mel in future. And as for Oliver Gladwyn, it was a bit of a coincidence those things happening at once: the disappearance of the daughter, and the family suddenly leaving Liverpool. Then there was the link to Puller and the murdered informant. And his thugs now harassing Jack's father. Investigating Oliver Gladwyn's links to Puller would very likely be fruitful, but Sarah had been firm—keep her husband out of it.

He got out his notebook and remembered Oliver Gladwyn's presentation. He checked his watch. He could still make it. There was even time to pick up a take-out coffee and toast after dropping Roy off.

CHAPTER SIXTEEN

'Walk out that door, ladies and gentlemen,' Oliver Gladwyn pointed, and every face in the audience, maybe five hundred of them, turned to follow his finger, 'and you're on the Liverpool waterfront. River Mersey, Irish Sea, Atlantic Ocean. The UK is surrounded by seas with the biggest and fastest tides in the world. If we're going to meet the government's climate change targets, we need to think radical and think big. The seas could provide us with most of the renewable energy we need, whether it's from wind, waves or barrages ...'

Jack Gordon looked around the hall. Not your typical conference room—exposed wood and brick; soaring ceiling; glass; view out over the Mersey to the Wirral; the Clwyd hills beyond, under an overcast sky.

'Note the word "most", ladies and gentlemen. I and my colleagues on the steering committee accept that you can't rely on one renewable energy source and that the country has to have a mix, whether its wind, solar, gas and even nuclear.'

Boos from the back of the hall.

'Yes, nuclear,' Gladwyn said with a grin. 'For a time. We suggest that nuclear be phased out over a number of years as our proposals come online. The key fact to understand about barrages is that the tides wait for no man. In out, twice a day. Through light and dark, calm sky and no wind, international oil and gas crises and reactor meltdowns. No.' He wafted his hand slowly back and forwards. 'In, out. In, out.' Titters from the audience. 'And the other key fact to understand is that after the initial capital outlay, the energy is free for a hundred years. And if you design it well, virtually no ongoing maintenance. And, of course, no decontamination bill at the end. What's not to like?'

'What about the environment!' A young, bearded man jumped out of his seat near the front. 'It'll mess up the estuary, just when the Mersey has been given a clean bill of health!'

'Thank you,' Gladwyn said, his voice earnest now. 'That's exactly the reason that the previous scheme was knocked on the head. Well, we've talked to the fishermen and the naturalists, and we propose a series of fish ladders so the salmon, trout, eels and the rest can easily pass through the barrage. It's all shown in the plans on display. And, crucially, we propose to create a lagoon that will support waders and nesting birds, similar to the one created when they built the road tunnels at Conway. I've been and talked to the fishermen and the bird watchers myself and explained our new proposals. They accept that it's a big improvement. And with the recent changes to interest rates, we can now interest international investors and convince them that it is a good place to put their money.'

'Exactly!' Everyone's head turned to the figure standing at the back of the hall who'd yelled the word out at the top of his voice. 'Exactly! It'll make money for international capitalists who are going to develop the sites you open up. There are hardly any jobs in it once it's constructed. Why not go for solar panels on every roof in the country and insulation for every wall?'

'As you well know, Brian, but prefer to forget, the sunlight levels in this country aren't high, and the sun doesn't always shine. Maybe some clever scientist could work out a way of getting energy from rainfall. Then we'd be on to something. The north west of England would become like a Gulf oil state.'

Laughter from the audience.

'Yeah,' the questioner said, his head held to one side and a smile on his face. 'What about the access to the development land that'll be opened up? You haven't mentioned that. Who's going to profit from that? Maybe Mersey Estates? Your new partners, appointed with no competitive tenders?'

Gladwyn just grinned at this. 'Any more questions?' He pointed to a man in the front row with his hand up.

'John East. About this fish ladder ...'

Jack had been examining the plan on the overhead. It had taken him some time to work out exactly where the site was.

Someone tapped his shoulder. He turned to be met by the grinning face of Ben Tyrer.

'Hi, Jack,' Tyrer whispered. 'How's the wanking going?'

Jack smiled back. *Don't be provoked.*

'So,' Tyrer said, still whispering, 'what's an ex copper like you doing in a place like this.'

'I'm interested in the environment, Ben, saving the planet.' He looked Tyrer up and down. His greased-back hair had 'almost a mullet' at the back, and his dark blue, pin-stripe suit was too smart for a detective.

Tyrer belched.

A woman sitting in a seat in front turned and glared at them.

'You look like you're doing well for yourself,' Jack said, trying hard to keep his voice down. 'In fact, you look like a Burton's dummy.'

'Yeah, when I made detective inspector I thought I'd better smarten up. Look the part and all that.'

Jack whistled. The lady in front stiffened. 'DI?' Jack said.

'Yep, it's my job to keep an eye on the low-lifes in this great city of ours.' He looked Jack up and down, a big grin on his face.

'Don't be like that, Ben. We used to be colleagues—remember?' He wondered whether or not to ask if Tyrer had anything to do with the covering up of Sally Parker's supposed suicide. But, no, best not provoke him.

'I remember.' Tyrer's voice was a whisper, but the tone was hard. 'And just you remember this, Flash fucking Gordon; you stick to harassing benefits claimants and your divorce cases and all the rest of your bottom-feeding stuff.'

Jack stiffened with rage but, before he could respond, Tyrer went on: 'If I catch you operating on our turf without our knowledge, I'll close you down so fast the stitches will pop on that conk of yours and you'll suddenly find yourself sitting in Church Street rattling a tin for spare change.'

The lady in front turned, and, like a cinema goer chastising noisy teenagers, said: 'This is important! I'm trying to listen to this!'

'And so, ladies and gentlemen,' Gladwyn said, 'if you'd like to help yourselves to some refreshments ...' He pointed to a table laden with cups and saucers and plates of sandwiches and cakes, behind which stood a couple of smiling waitresses.

Jack joined the queue which quickly formed, being careful to keep his distance from Tyrer. Any more cracks from him and Jack might do something he might regret, like striking an officer of the law in front of a hundred witnesses. Probably exactly what Tyrer wanted.

The man in front half turned. Jack couldn't catch the man's name on his tag, but he noticed *The Guardian*. He tapped the man's shoulder. 'Hi,' he said. 'I see you're from *The Guardian*.'

'Yeah,' the man said. 'Alan Southern. We're planning a feature on Vince Gladwyn. How do you think the presentation went?'

Jack laughed. 'It all sounds fine in these presentations, but it seems like there's some opposition. The bird watchers and the fishermen always object, don't they?'

'It's not so much them that's the problem with this project,' Southern said. 'It's the finance. Without government support it's not going anywhere.' He paused. 'And all these accusations don't help. It would make a nice investigative story. I was about to organise an interview with Gladwyn. It's a shame, I was looking forward to meeting him, but I've just been called back to London. Boris has dropped one again.'

'So what's new?' Jack laughed. 'I say, have you got a card?'

'Sure.' Southern handed one over. Jack put in the top pocket of his jacket.

A loud 'crump' sound came from outside, heavy but muffled.

*

Jack slumped into the driver's seat and slammed the car door. Two cops were cordoning off the end of the car park where the four-by-four Mercedes belonging to Oliver Gladwyn still smouldered under the watchful eye of a fireman. Someone had been seen next to the car before it caught alight and had run off into the woods pursued by a security man. Jack heard the thump-thump of a helicopter overhead. A white van screeched to a halt in the car park and half a dozen coppers and a couple of dogs piled out.

Jack started the engine and drove off, leaving them to it. He turned on the radio, just in time for a newsflash:

> *A car was set on fire outside the new conference centre on the Dock Road where a presentation of the revised Mersey barrage proposals was being made. A suspect believed to be Freddie Devon, also known as Freddie the Ferret, a well-known anarchist activist wanted for a series of attacks in the Bristol area, was pursued into woods by police. Police are treating this as a terrorist attack and have warned the public not to approach the suspect as he may be dangerous.*

The news moved onto President Trump's latest Twitter gaffe, and Jack turned the thing off before he could be told on which country Trump had declared war.

Freddie Devon? Freddie the fucking Ferret? No, it couldn't be.

He'd known Freddie Devon at Bristol University where Jack had read Economics and Politics. Freddie had been a law student. He'd had short hair and a conventional appearance. Jack remembered a party at Freddie's house with lots of dope being smoked. The police had raided the party, and Jack had escaped over the back fence—he had ambitions to join the police and didn't want to get caught up in it. Freddie cut the side of his face on broken glass while trying to get through a window, he'd nearly bled to death. They'd charged him with dealing and given him a short prison sentence, ruining his career—you can't be a lawyer if you have a criminal record. Jack could've come forward and argued Freddie's innocence, but he was worried that he might've been dragged into it.

He pulled into the car park by his flat and turned in the seat to reverse into a space. A movement in the back of the car caught his eye and a bespectacled face appeared, the head bald at the front with long hair at the back.

'Freddie,' Jack said. 'It must be fifteen years.'

The face cracked into a smile, and Jack caught a glimpse of the edge of the puckered pale-coloured scar. 'More like eighteen.'

CHAPTER SEVENTEEN

'So what do you people believe?' Jack said. 'Or is it just burning down banks at the G20 … or burning Chelsea tractors in car parks?'

He took a sip of his whisky. Glenmorangie—he'd been saving it for a special occasion. The warmth of the alcohol spread through his body. He'd managed to spirit Freddie into the flat away from Harry's watchful eyes. Then he'd thrown some oven chips and two pieces of battered fish into the oven, and two packs of mushy peas into the microwave. Not much of a meal, but at least it wasn't from the chippy. And Freddie had tucked in with gusto. Jack made a mental note to improve his diet. He leaned back in the armchair, relaxed now. The heat had abated with nightfall, and with the windows open, it was reasonably cool in the lounge.

Freddie laughed and shook his head, his long hair flicking as he did so, giving a glimpse of the scar. 'We're actually opposed to violence, and we resort to it only as a last resort.' He looked at Jack's nose. 'So who gave you that? Was it a last resort?'

'An accident.' Jack laughed. 'Well, those guys at those protests seem to have a good time, destroying things. I bet the people who really suffer if a bank is burned down aren't the big men at the top but the people who work on the desks and the cleaners, security men, people on minimum wage.'

'The G20 is the ultimate form of government. It's almost a world government. The world's twenty richest countries. It represents the oppression of people by international capitalism.'

'You sound like Wolfie Smith, the urban guerrilla,' Jack said. 'Remember him?' He raised a fist. 'Power to the people!'

Freddie giggled. 'That's the image portrayed by the capitalist press. Anarchists throwing bombs. We abhor violence. We always give warnings so innocent people aren't hurt.' He tilted his head and watched Jack carefully. 'You might know something about hurting innocent people.'

'What do you mean by that?'

Both of them knew exactly to what he was referring but neither seemed to want to be the first to raise the subject.

After a long silence, Jack shook his head. 'Well, if you use violence, things always go wrong,' he said. 'The warning doesn't get through or the bomb goes off prematurely. Look at all those IRA bombings that went wrong. In any case, if you were being attacked by a gang of fascist thugs, you'd be happy for the police to rescue you. You're just hypocrites.'

'The police further the state's coercion of ordinary people. Granted they feel criminals' collars and suchlike, but they also perform a more sinister role.'

'That's true to a certain extent, but all this stuff about fighting the state, the government; they actually do a lot of good things, like pay unemployment benefit, run the health service.'

'We're not against those things. They could be provided by people agreeing amongst themselves. It's the coerciveness of the system that we're against. Our strategy is to influence public opinion. We realise that it will take years for true anarchy to prevail. What we want is for people to question authority and hold it to account; for people more and more to take control of their own lives and their own locality.'

He took a sip of whisky. 'Look, Jack,' he went on. 'Are you happy with being a cog in a bureaucratic machine? With your thoughts, feelings and tastes manipulated by government and industry and the mass communications they control? At one time they pushed the line that smoking ciggies was harmless and even good for you. It was all secretly funded by tobacco companies. Now they question the very existence of climate change and the coming ecological disaster and encourage us to consume more and more.'

'Well, obviously I don't want that, no-one who isn't an idiot would want that. I just don't see how blowing up police cars and burning down banks is going to change things.'

Neither said anything for a few moments.

'In any case,' Jack continued, 'what have you got against Oliver Gladwyn? Isn't a barrage a clean source of energy, good for the planet? After all, he's changed the project to address the environmental concerns.'

'We don't like Gladwyn because he's a capitalist in hippie clothing. Making Wirral Wanderers into a vegan football team? Do me a favour. All that investment would be better going into wind or solar or insulating homes. Did you know that he's got nasty things in his past?'

'What, like the Welsh water thing? Isn't this just getting your own back on what that family did to your dad?'

'That's part of it. I realise that Gladwyn married into that family well after all those criminal actions had been carried out; I'll concede that. Though they hurt my family.'

'Care to expand on that?'

'No.' Freddie looked away, avoiding eye contact. 'I don't want to.' He snapped his head back, took off his glasses and stared Jack straight in the eye. 'But did you know that he made his money peddling drugs? The rumour is that he killed an informer. Or had him killed. And the electricity from the barrage is only part of it. It's actually quite difficult to make that pay. No, the real money comes from the land the barrage opens up. If you look at the plans carefully, you'll see that there's a link road from each end of the barrage to a nearby dual carriageway or motorway, and that takes a bit of a circuitous route. A bit like a bypass around a town that's in the green belt. You get to develop the land between the bypass and the town. That's where the real money is.' He laughed. 'It's basic town and country planning, mate. Typical capitalist smoke and mirrors scam. It looks on the surface like a project that's going to save the planet, but really it opens up land for development. Exceedingly lucrative development. '

'Okay, so what was this stuff about Helen Gladwyn's disappearance?'

Freddie nodded thoughtfully. 'My cousin, Eric Owen, worked for the Gladwyns as a chauffeur in the summer she disappeared. The stories he told me when he'd had a few. Eric wasn't your typical Welshman like me—small and dark, almost a midget. No, he was big and blonde, more like a typical English ploughboy. Started off doing odd jobs for the Gladwyns and then became their chauffeur. Oliver Gladwyn and Johnny Puller were in a rock band—a poor man's Led Zeppelin, really. Parties, drugs, sex, the lot. The lifestyle without the Led

Zepp's talent. Did you know that old man Gladwyn knew Aleister Crowley?'

'What, The Beast?'

'That was all character assassination by the right-wing press. He wasn't that bad. Anyway, he used to stay at their big house. Must have influenced young Oliver and Johnny. They had this wild party at the house the Gladwyns had in Liverpool. Eric helped out with serving the drinks and the food. The things he told me went on, you wouldn't believe.'

He paused for effect and took another sip of his whisky. 'Anyway, one or the other must have come on to Helen too hard. Something happened; I'm not sure what. She was supposed to have disappeared. Clothes found by the river. Looked like suicide—or made to look like suicide. It was covered up. The Gladwyns had contacts with the authorities. Something about it stinks, mate.'

After a long silence, Freddie said, 'I know all about what happened back at uni, Jack.' His voice was low and carried a hint of sadness and regret. 'A friend worked for the police as a civilian and heard about it. You shopped me to save yourself?'

Jack opened his mouth, but no words came out.

Freddie continued, 'Technically, I was in the wrong, allowing my house to be used for smoking dope. But tell me a party in those days that didn't have people smoking dope. Was I supposed to be a policeman, as it were, going around confiscating joints and baccy tins full of shit and Rizla papers? The thing was, Jack, you were my mate. You legged it out of the back window, but the rozzers nabbed you, and then you shopped me to save your pathetic little future career as a copper yourself. But I was in the last year of a Law degree. And, of course, if you have a criminal conviction you can't be a lawyer. In fact, it's difficult to get any sort of job. So I bummed around sleeping on floors, smoking shit—the usual. Though I never dropped as far as the needle.' He took a deep breath.

Jack stared at the wall.

'Then one day I was lying in bed,' Freddie continued, 'at twelve o'clock in the day and thinking about my dad who was thrown in the clink on some grass's word. The idiots blew up a water pipe in Cheshire. Can you imagine it? No one hurt, a few hundred pounds' worth of damage, but he was sent to jail. He had issues with depression and topped himself. I'd been talking to some people in Anarchy UK, and I'd read up about the Sons of Glyndwr so here I am.'

All this was sinking in with Jack. He'd known that Freddie was a Taff from North Wales but with only a trace of an accent. They'd always had good-natured banter when Wales played England at Rugby, but Freddie had never referred to his family or his upbringing.

Freddie grinned at Jack and motioned with his glass.

*

'And your nickname is Flash Gordon.'

How did she know that? Dr fucking Eastman in the so professional blue suit.

'That's right. I'm a bit of a flashy character.'

'Making up for being Billy-No-Mates at school?'

'Well that's a bit of an obvious one if I may say so.'

'I know, but this is about your persona. The image you present to the world. Not your real self.'

He shrugged. 'Everyone wants to present a good face to the world. It's human nature.'

'Exactly.' She made a note. 'Now we must deal with the anima and the animus.'

'Ah yes,' Jack said. 'The anima and the animus. The feminine side of the male and the male side of the feminine. What a load of bollocks.'

'So you've been reading up on the subject.'

'Yes, I have. If I was paying for this myself, I'd have to have been out of here by now. There's not that much difference between men and women. Same wants and desires. Same cruelties and kindnesses. In my experience they're much the same. A few hormones here, a dick there, a pair of tits … sorry, but you said don't hold back …'

'We're getting some hostility here …'

'Yes, we are. I'll be the first to admit that women should be paid the same as men and not have to wear high heels to work—all that equality stuff—not be a handmaid in some misogynist tale, but some women want more than their share.'

121

'I beg to disagree, Jack. Women want to be equal but different, exactly the same as if they were from a different race or culture, but not the same as if gender equality were some mathematical equation that always provides the answer fifty-fifty.'

'So what about all this deep stuff, the anima, animus nonsense?'

'Well, let's get down to it.'

Jack settled back in his seat and consciously clenched and unclenched his fists, trying to relax. Fuck! He was falling in love with the condescending bitch!

'My initial thoughts are these: your father made fun of your female side, your anima, and you were an over-sensitive, lonely child, prone to guilt. Not exactly in line with your persona of the hard-boiled cop stroke private investigator. Do you recall the Woody Allen film Play it Again Sam? In which the wimp is given advice by a ghostly Humphrey Bogart?'

'One of my favourite films. "I never met a dame that didn't understand a smack in the mouth or a slug from a forty-five."' He managed to reproduce the Bogart lisp on the words 'forty-five'.

'Exactly. A comedy, but with the ring of truth. To be honest there's nothing wrong with a man being oversensitive. Not such a bad thing at all. We need more people like you in the world.'

It was meant to be a compliment, but Jack wasn't so sure. If over-sensitivity and being guilt-prone in the male represented the anima, did hardness and being violent represent the animus in the female? Wouldn't that be just going around in circles?

'I think, Jack, that we are reaching a positive conclusion in this analysis. We'll finally deal with synchronicity.'

Jack thought he'd heard of the concept, and he'd heard of Sting's rock album. It sounded a bit trendy. 'Meaningful coincidences?' he ventured.

'Got it in one. But I must ask you something.'

'Go ahead.'

'Have you been completely honest? Have you told me the truth?'

Long pause.

'Completely.'

CHAPTER EIGHTEEN

Alan couldn't remember the explosion itself. Just the aftermath. Thirst. Always thirsty in the desert, what with the heat and the dust and the smell of death, but this was different. Throat and mouth totally dry. Lips stuck together so he couldn't shout for help. No pain. That came later. Greyness everywhere. Silence and grey dust. His eyes itching with the dust. Grey dust. Sam, the driver, was groaning and whispering something, the same thing over and over. Alan couldn't make it out.

Someone tried to flush the toilet in the next cubicle. It gurgled and hiccupped but didn't flush. God, it was hot in here. And it stunk. Flies buzzing everywhere. Disgusting.

A voice exclaimed: 'Jesus wept! The bog don't flush! Why do I always get the bog that don't flush!' A door crashed shut, and Alan leapt from his seat, knocking over his stick and sending a spasm through his right leg. It took a while to pull himself together so he could sit down again, his damp bum cheeks making a squelching sound.

Woolly back. Probably one of the ones from St Helens. Alan had been raised on a corpy estate in Whiston, not far from where Stevey Gerard had been brought up. It was on the border between the woolly-backs and the scousers. And Alan was one of the scousers. They'd had many a good gang fight with bricks and sticks. Later knives, baseball bats and pistols. Happy days.

He wished he could be back now with his mum, living in the back room of her little corpy house. She was kind but had to manage on her old age pension, but with his army pension, though not exactly rich, they could live comfortably. He couldn't wish himself back with his family, though, what with his nightmares, waking up screaming in the middle of the night. And popping pills all the time. And his problems with the pop itself. And overreacting to loud noises. No, best ease his way back into normal life, get a job, keep with the therapy and become a normal member of the human race.

The idea of the training scheme was to rehabilitate you, so you could hold down a job and look after yourself. Great in principle, but he was still in pain from his back. Couldn't sleep. And when he did nod off, he had strange nightmares. Even now he could feel his back starting to kick off.

He checked his watch. Nearly the end of the lunch break. Back soon to learning how to lay bricks with that tosser, Hargreaves. Laying bricks wasn't exactly rocket science, was it? Set out your line with the spirit level. Butter the brick with mortar. Place it. Get it square, working by eye. If it looks right, it is right. And what was it Hargreaves had been going on about that morning? Plasticiser. Mixing it into the mortar makes it easier to work.

He remembered that his dad had been trained as a bricklayer after the Second World War. It made sense. Cities like Liverpool needed to be rebuilt. Nowadays it was just a dead-end manual job. Once you picked up the basics—how to use the line; how to butter the bricks and lay them like a machine—that was it. It wouldn't be long before they invented a brick-laying machine and then he'd be out of a job.

He'd have preferred to go into computers—every soldier did a bit of that in the modern army—but there were no places. He closed his eyes. One last memory. After the air strike—U.S. air strike, the bastards.

He'd rubbed his eyes and managed to get them open a crack. Sam, the driver, was lying with his mouth open—big yellow teeth; lolling tongue; eyes closed; face grey with dust. He was trying to say something. Alan tried to make it out but couldn't. Just a croak.

They'd been protecting the flank of the Yanks—bodies, fire, smoke; hard to see. American bulldozers flattened trenches with Iraqi soldiers still in them. They were hit just after noon. F15s firing

Maverick anti-tank missiles, as he'd discovered later. It was on YouTube now like a computer game. He couldn't watch the videos. Once you knew that it was real flesh and blood being ripped and burnt down there, it was different.

The F15 pilots had thought they were Iraqi T-72s counterattacking. A Warrior's profile is nothing like a T-72 even from fifteen-thousand feet. Except a Warrior has a lot thinner armour than a T-72. The missile went through the Warriors' armour like a hot knife through Lurpak. It wasn't all one-sided. A US Black Hawk chopper was shot down by a British ant-aircraft missile. Just like in the film Black Hawk Down. A shambles. And all for oil and money. Would they have gone to war for carrots? Not fucking likely.

Then the hospital. The Iraqi hospital was pretty basic, though they treated him well enough, considering. And then the pain. He'd seen the movies where the wounded soldier is given morphine and a cigarette and lies with a lazy grin on his face, all relaxed and happy. But for this pain they couldn't find anything that worked— not morphine, codeine, tramadol, fentanyl or any of the others he couldn't remember. Even penicillin and the other anti-biotics didn't work now on account of the bugs building up resistance from farmers feeding it to pigs. They sold it over the counter in Pakistan. People ate it like sweets and that's how resistance started.

They treated him well when he was captured. And the people from the other place. They must have drugged him because he couldn't remember a thing apart from vague recollections of a hospital room, all gleaming white and modern—nothing like the ramshackle medical facilities the Iraqis used.

Then he woke in a different hospital bed with the nurses speaking English. Back in Blighty. The doctors found a cocktail that worked on the pain, and he was put through six months of healing and rehabilitation. At the end he had therapy to improve movement, but the uncontrollable pain started again. At one point he'd screamed to the doctors and nurses, 'Just cut the fuckers off!' Which was daft as the pain in his legs came from the damaged nerves in his back. Most of the other casualties at Selly Oak had missing limbs. They usually had mental issues as well. So Alan was lucky compared to them. And they did have some good laughs putting a brave face on it.

The good thing about the army was the comradeship. You cared for your mates and they cared for you. Like Sam, the ginger driver. Shared many a pint and a story. Sam was from Scotland. Glasgow. Thickest accent you ever heard. Like a foreign tongue. Eventually, Alan had managed to work out most of what Sam was saying.

'Ah wiznah' meant 'I wasn't', and 'ya beg wee-an' meant 'you big baby'.

Lying in the greyness inside the wrecked
Warrior in the Iraqi desert, Alan could just make out
what Sam was whispering:
        'Water!'

CHAPTER NINETEEN

'Sorry to drop on you like this, but I was in the area to sort out this business with the Range Rover, so I thought I'd pop in for a chat.'

Even though she'd just come in from the oppressive heat outside, Sarah Gladwyn looked so cool that Jack could imagine his fingers sticking to her face if he touched her. Touched her? As if. She was the Ice Maiden. Hitchcock would've loved her, put her opposite Jimmy Stewart—wine-coloured, tight-fitting leather jacket; well-cut jeans with calf length black high-heeled boots; hair tied back; exquisite.

'It's no trouble,' Jack said, leaning back in his chair and trying to appear relaxed. He'd made sure the air con was working and sprayed the interview room with air freshener. No chippy smells. 'Particularly for such an attractive client as yourself.'

She laughed. 'Careful, Mr Gordon, you're not supposed to talk like that to women these days.'

'I'm afraid I'm a bit old-fashioned. If a lady's about to step into a puddle, I'll take my coat off and put it over the water. Don't want to get wet feet, do we?'

She laughed, louder this time, and her green eyes sparkled. 'Bravo! I heard that you were a ladies' man. What do they call you, Flash Gordon?'

'Among other things.' He couldn't exactly tell the truth about Freddie. That when he'd woken up in the morning, Freddie was gone. Best keep the whole episode with Freddie quiet for now. And Jack would've been seen at the presentation. He'd have to make it up as he went along. 'I suppose you want to know what happened with the Range Rover. We've tried everything in the book, but unfortunately some things aren't in the book. Though we're pretty sure that it was Freddie the Ferret who torched your car at the presentation.'

'You were there?'

He nodded.

'So where do we go from here?'

'We have our methods. The problem is that I don't think we've got the full picture. Like this Johnny Puller who seems to have some sort of hold over your husband. He's buying up development land that'll be worth a bomb when this barrage is built.'

She said nothing.

'And these skeletons in the cupboard that Freddie goes on about in his letters?' he added.

'The man's got a grudge against our family. His father was given a jail sentence for blowing up a water pipeline and died there. Not exactly our fault. And his grandfather led a strike in the quarries and lost his job. It wasn't very pleasant, but that was my ancestors. Nothing to do with me.'

'What strikes me is that he knows a lot about your family. Did anyone from his family work in any of your houses, as a domestic servant, maybe?'

She thought for a moment. 'Not that I know of.'

'Devon, it's not a common Welsh name, is it? Might be worth checking.' Jack made a note.

She got up and walked over to the window. 'I'll be candid with you, Mr Gordon,' she said over her shoulder as she stared out of the window. 'There are some terrible secrets in my family.'

'You mean the disappearance of your sister?'

'That's just one of them,' she said, without turning. 'I suppose you've checked out our family secrets?'

'We always check out our clients. We were taken to the cleaners in the early days trusting plausible people who turned out to be crooks.' He paused. 'Not that I'm saying that you are … What I mean is … You don't have to talk about it.'

'No, I want to. Me and Oliver were not long married.' She laughed. 'Sorry, Oliver and I. I'm forgetting my expensive education. Johnny was Oliver's best mate. I knew they were travellers together, pushed dope and that kind of thing. They were in a rock band. It was glamorous to a young girl of twenty. We had this party in the lodge to the main house. Things got a bit wild; you know, drugs, alcohol, sex. Oliver caught Johnny with my kid sister. Big bust up. She stormed out. Took a taxi to the station to go back to Wales. Then she disappeared off the face of the earth. Her clothes were found in a neat pile just along from the Pierhead.' She reached for her bag by the side of the chair, took out a hankie and dabbed her eyes, then she sat down and looked Jack full in the face.

'No one disappears off the face of the earth,' Jack said. 'Didn't the police ...'

'The police? Useless bastards. No, it's a mystery to this day. Look, Mr Gordon ...'

'What's with all this Mr Gordon business? Call me Jack.'

She smiled. Full of charm and grace. 'I prefer Mr Gordon. Look, I want you to investigate my sister's disappearance, using all your unconventional methods. The conventional ones were worthless.'

'What about Freddie the Ferret and his merry chums?'

'That as well. I have this feeling that there's some connection.'

'What? That Freddie had something to do with your sister's disappearance?'

'Yes.'

'What about your husband and Johnny Puller? If they were at that party, then they might have some clues about what happened.'

She turned away. 'I would prefer it if you didn't involve Oliver directly.'

'And Puller?'

'Discreetly. He has some sort of hold over Oliver, something from the old days. I could never stand the man. I know they were involved in drugs. At first, I thought it was glamorous, but I soon realised that it was more than a couple of students pushing a bit of dope. And something happened in Australia. I'm not sure what—I think they nearly got caught—but then they moved into legitimate activity. Separately. I'd like to see a complete dossier on this change, and why they did it separately.'

Jack sighed. He'd have to discuss this with Mel. Probably he'd have to take on Oliver since investigating him would need careful handling to comply with Sarah's wishes. Though Puller was by far the most dangerous of the two. This would need some careful thought.

'You look like you want to ask a question,' she said.

He opened his mouth to speak, but she cut him off.

'Look, Mr Gordon. This is confidential. I've asked my husband for a divorce, and he's quibbling about how much he's worth.' She sighed. 'So I need a breakdown of his wealth. And Mr Puller's, if it comes to that, as he's now my husband's business partner and part of the equation.'

'Presumably you've tried Companies House and all the usual sources of information?'

'They're clever. Everything is laundered, hidden and salted away.' She paused, letting all this sink in.

'This might turn out to be expensive,' he said at last.

'Money's no object, Jack ... Mr Gordon.'

CHAPTER TWENTY

'Well, at least Roy is working from home,' Jack said. He watched Mel closely, but she just raised an eyebrow and kept on shuffling the papers in the file in front of her.

The air conditioning had cooled the room down and they could keep the windows closed, so there was no smell of frying chips.

'Okay,' Jack said. 'I'll start.' He pressed the *record* button on the tape machine—Lucy was too busy to take notes and could do it later. 'Our client, Sarah Gladwyn, has asked us to investigate the business affairs of Oliver Gladwyn and Johnny Puller and, in particular, their move into legit business activity from drug dealing, and the laundering of cash that this entailed.' He pressed a button on the laptop and a scene unfolded on the screen on the wall. 'This is the Snug as a Bug factory in Ellesmere Port.'

Mel whistled. The factory was big and modern, not more than ten years old. White cladding with the 'Snug as a Bug' logo in red. The letters must have been ten feet high.

'They started off with double glazing,' Jack continued. 'For many businesses, cash flow is a problem, that is, a lack of cash, but for your average drug-dealing outfit, the problem is too much cash, usually dirty fivers and tenners in Tesco carrier bags.'

He laughed. 'At one time you filled a duffel bag with all the spare readies,' he said, 'and sent a bagman down on the train to a Bureau de Change in London to change it into clean money. But the bizzies are onto that now. So what you do is buy a failing legitimate business—in this case double glazing—for a song. Then you use your spare dosh to, for instance, pay cash in hand or to give salesmen bonuses. This gives you an edge over your competitors. Everything else is legit: tax; national insurance; working conditions; union membership; you name it. No hard sell practices, like most of the competition, so you get a reputation as a trustworthy business. And double-glazing saves money on heating bills and helps to save the planet, so you think about this and move into insulating houses with government grants and then into the big one: solar panels. And before you know it, you're a famous eco warrior.' He paused. 'That's what we know about Oliver Gladwyn's business activities. Your turn.'

Mel laughed. 'That business model is kinda familiar,' she said. 'Except Johnny Puller's was a bit more down to earth and dirty. Though he ended up with a string of fancy estate agent's offices.' She unplugged Jack's laptop, plugged in her own and pressed a button. A photo appeared of two shop units on a suburban street with the *Mersey Estates* sign across them—strangely, red on white, like *Snug as a Bug*. Another photo showed a shop interior of subtle lighting and oak flooring, and rack after rack of house details. 'He started off with security companies— traditionally cash in hand—but that came to an end with the Jamaica Jim affair.'

'Jamaica Jim? The feller who chopped up his wife with a machete?'

'Yeah, he was manager of Cherry Tree Security. His wife caught him with a fancy woman while he was on the job, so to speak. Too much publicity.' She shook her head. 'Only in Liverpool. They put everything they had into construction. Great way to get rid of readies from grubby hands into clean ones; no questions asked, despite the close attention of the authorities since *The Boys from the Black Stuff* shone a light on it. You buy a rundown property with readies, do it up with your cash-in-hand labour force, sell on and start again. Before long, your cash is laundered two or three times. And the point about cash in hand is that it's in the employee's interests to keep quiet. And if anyone gets to think about opening their mouths, you still have your gangland connections to shut them up. And, eventually, you've got an estates empire that's totally legit, like the double-glazing outfit, paying all taxes and bills on time. In fact, making a point of paying all taxes and bills on time.'

'Precisely,' Jack said. 'But because it's cash in hand, there's no audit trail. And if your potential witnesses are complicit in the fraud and too scared to speak out, you've no chance of a conviction. And even if it goes to court, all that money buys you a crack team of lawyers. I mean, OJ Simpson was caught literally red-handed, and he got off.'

So,' Mel said after thinking about this. 'We're fucked.'

'That about sums it up. The interesting thing about this job, though, is that Oliver and Puller obviously fell out about something before they both decided to get out of the drug dealing and went their separate ways. But somehow Puller convinced Oliver to make him his business partner in this development associated with Oliver's pet project, the barrage. It must have been something powerful to make him change his mind.'

'Something like a murder that you could use to blackmail him.'

'Precisely.'

'What about the anarchists and the water terrorists?' Mel said.

Jack shrugged. 'Freddie and his crew will have to go on the back burner for the time being. Maybe Roy will come up with something on the water boys.'

She snorted, but he was now deep in thought.

'There's only one way to move on with this …' he said at last.

'And I bet that way involves physical risk to my arse.'

'And mine.'

'Work inside?'

CHAPTER TWENTY-ONE

Oliver Gladwyn was smaller, older and greyer than in his media images and the impression he'd given at a lectern above an audience. Probably true for most celebrities, Jack thought. The most common Gladwyn media shot seemed to be on a yacht in high seas, the eco-warrior laughing into the wind, his face framed by a wildly tousled dark mane of hair. The romantic rebel personified.

At the moment, showing Jack to a seat outside the marina cafe, he seemed a bit preoccupied and irritable. At least a slight breeze blew off the Mersey, which made the heat bearable.

'Right!' he said when they'd seated themselves at a table. He seemed to be making an effort to snap out of a bad mood. 'You haven't worked for *The Guardian* long have you?'

'Two months; I'm still finding my feet.'

'Yes, I thought I hadn't seen your pic in the paper.' He checked what must be a briefing note in front of him. 'Alan Southern, Environment Correspondent. Well, fire away.' He stared at Jack's nose, no doubt wondering if *Guardian* reporters made a habit of sticking their conks where they shouldn't and getting them dobbed.

Jack pulled his notebook from his bag on the table. 'I suppose we could start with the obvious things first, Mr Gladwyn.'

'Call me Oliver, Alan.'

'Okay. Your chequered past, Oliver.' He laughed. 'Let's get that out of the way first.'

Gladwyn sighed. 'What? Being a traveller, rock star and marrying into aristocracy?'

'I know you're fed up with it, but it adds colour to a story for our readers. And they like a good story. So you were a traveller for many years, had a partner and three children—'

'For whom I pay through the nose every month.'

'Right. And before that you were in Creatures of Darkness, played with Led Zeppelin, and you were mates with Jimmy Page and Robert Plant.'

'Still play with them occasionally. Last time it was acoustic at the Cambridge Folk festival.'

Jack reached for his iPad and googled. 'Yes,' he laughed. 'There's a photo of the gig here. Might use that.'

'Feel free, mate.'

'Okay,' Jack said slowly. 'Now for the difficult bit: the wild parties; the drugs; the accusations of sex with underage girls; orgies stimulated by the ideas of Aleister Crowley; then the accusations of drug-dealing when you were travelling. I believe a witness disappeared under suspicious circumstances. I'm sorry to bring this stuff up, Oliver. But our readers are educated and informed, for all their faults. They'll know about these accusations.'

Gladwyn shrugged. 'Not at all. I expected this. All I can say is that I've smoked a lot of weed and dropped a lot of acid in my time, but I've never served a day in jail for shagging underage girls, drug dealing or murder. The stuff about orgies and Crowley is a *Daily Mail* lie. They assassinated Crowley's reputation to sell newspapers. When, in fact, if you read his books, he comes over as quite reasonable. And I tell you something else. Anyone who says that there is anything more in those accusations is pissing in the wind. In fact, the wind will turn the piss back into their faces when the letters from my solicitor land on the doormat.'

'Wow, that's good. Can I quote you on that?'

'By all means.'

'Okay, let's get onto the eco-warrior bit.'

'I thought you'd never ask.' He pointed. 'See that yacht over there, the one with the light-green hull?'

Jack looked over the rows of yachts—lots of bright pastel colours, the masts like the massed pikes of a medieval army. Beyond, the yellow-brick blocks of flats hemmed in the dock on three sides, the yellow brick broken with lines of darker, red-brown brick. The mass of the cathedral towered over the whole marina. To one side stood endless blocks of newly constructed flats for yuppies and students in red brick and plastic panels.

He identified the yacht—the largest in the marina. 'It looks like quite a boat.'

'You're not kidding, mister. The sails are actually solar panels. Can you believe it? Cutting edge technology. So as well as driving the boat, they provide us with energy for whatever we want. I'll give you spin out to sea. Maybe pop round to Portmeirion.' He took in Jack's expression. 'Only joking,' he said. 'Come and have a look.'

Jack followed him down to the quayside until they stood alongside the yacht.

'Built in the 30s in Holland,' Gladwyn said. 'I recently had her refitted. Don't ask how much. Diesel electric propulsion, though that's just for emergencies. The batteries recharge while we're sailing. And the DynaRig sails have soft solar panels built in. In total the batteries can hold a million watts of electricity. Totally sustainable. Zero emissions. State of the art.'

Oliver Gladwyn was obviously proud of his baby. He motioned to Jack and they walked on. 'Computer controlled. Built from carbon fibre—'

'Carbon fibre? It looks like wood.'

'It does, doesn't it? The hull shape is computer designed to give thirty percent lower fuel consumption, and the interior was refurbished using reclaimed or recycled materials.' He laughed. 'It ticks all the boxes, Alan.'

They walked back to the café. Once they sat down, Jack said, 'There's another thing, Oliver. Marrying into one of the big Welsh families with all the baggage from the past—slate mines, reservoirs and all that.'

'Before my time, mate.'

'Okay, so what about Wirral Wanderers? Solar panels on the roof of the stand. Making the players eat vegan food and wear plastic boots.'

'Most professional football players eat responsibly nowadays. It's not pies and six pints at half time now, you know. And the panels have brought the leccy bill right down. What's there not to like?'

'Okay, Okay. So tell me about this barrage. Is it a goer?'

'Of course it's a goer. As you know, the problem with them is getting planning permission and getting the finance for the initially high capital costs.'

'There's a lot of opposition ...'

'Which we've sorted out. We've incorporated a weir for fish to move upstream to breed and then come back to the sea. Can I tell you something, mate? A professor of economic geography wrote that no form of energy production comes without a cost. With gas, coal and oil, it's pollution and climate change. With nuclear it's safety and dealing with the waste. As I said on the telly recently, the tide comes in every day and goes out every day regardless of governments, kings, queens and dictators, and it's been doing that since the time of King Canute.'

'Okay, so what about the finance and the planning permission?'

'I had a meeting with James Whitaker, the MP for this area, yesterday, and he promised me his support. We're also supported by all the councils and mayors, bless their little cotton socks. We're expecting government approval any day now.'

'Isn't it turning out to be a bit of a grind? All this effort. All the setbacks.'

Gladwyn's face changed, and for a moment Jack caught a glimpse of the real Oliver Gladwyn. He grinned at Jack and slapped his thighs. 'It's the future, Mr Southern, the future.' His expression changed again, suddenly serious. 'When it comes down to it, mate,' he said. 'It's all about saving the planet before it's too late. Now ask yourself, is that a worthy objective or is that a worthy objective?'

Jack nodded. He quite liked this guy.

CHAPTER TWENTY TWO

The big fascia sign stood out in the row of suburban shops. It stretched across three shop units knocked into one. Black and purple on white, just like the signs that had proliferated across the city like an infectious disease. 'Mersey Estates!' it proclaimed. 'We're new, we're brash and we're taking over!'

Inside, though, Mel could see that it was the usual real oak flooring, bright lighting and purple and black leather sofas, every inch of wall space covered by property details. Identical-looking, blonde female salespersons sat behind the desks.

Mel paused for a moment outside. She wore her best summer outfit—a cream-coloured suit with a white blouse—one so expensive she only brought it out for special occasions, like impressing clients, and cooler than her dark-blue number two outfit. She felt happy with her image, but what about Safe n' Secure's image? So tatty and rundown. If they were going to make a go of it, they needed to put forward a totally professional impression. It should be more like this one: Mersey Estates. Though she had to be careful not to push too hard. Sure, she'd run her own business, but it was Jack's show. Take it one step at a time.

She opened the door. At least here it was air-conditioned and cool inside.

Johnny Puller came bounding into the reception area. He cut an impressive figure for a man who must be into his fifties: over six feet tall with a Premiership target man's musculature; glossy black hair tied back in a bun; grey silk suit and a gleaming-white open-necked shirt. His grin showed a perfect Hollywood smile. Mel was gob smacked. Just her type. But she'd have to be careful. This man had been involved in the disappearance of an informer. He was as dangerous as a hungry Great White Shark.

'Jane! So nice to meet you!'

Mel caught a strong blast of some poncy perfume as he embraced her, a little too eagerly, and then kissed her on each cheek. The salesperson clones raised their eyebrows and giggled.

'Come on!' he said. 'We'll go straight out and have a look at the site if that's okay.'

Puller went down slightly in her estimation when she saw the number plate *PULL1* on the shiny black Porsche sports car. She got in, and they tore through the streets of suburban Liverpool. She was acutely aware of how close they were and how the reclined seats made her skirt rise up. Mentally she practised the role she'd made up for herself: Jane Forrester, site agent for a big investment company, on the lookout for a major retail opportunity in the Merseyside area. She'd run a property refurbishment business herself, and she hoped she had enough knowledge to blag it. And the car's air conditioning worked a treat.

They drove onto a dual carriageway—Aigburth Road. After a few hundred yards Puller pointed. 'Here we are. This is the start of the site. The planning consent stipulates that we come off an improved road access here. Easy access to south Liverpool with over a hundred-thousand well-off consumers. Huge untapped market.'

'So this planning consent is for the development site?' she said. 'It's different to the one for the barrage?'

'Yep!' He laughed. 'That's the hard one—satisfying the fishermen and the twitchers. The development site presses all the buttons, especially the one marked "jobs".'

Mel got out her mobile and snapped a few shots from the car. 'Can we stop and have a look around?' she said.

'By all means.' Puller parked in a layby and they walked a few yards to the entrance to what looked like parkland.

'Wasn't this the garden festival site?' she said as they walked in.

'Sure was. We'll keep part of it to serve as public open space for the new houses, but there's a huge swathe down by the river that'll be opened up for commercial development by the new barrage.'

Mel wondered about the parkland, playing fields and allotments that must be incorporated into the development site but decided not to say anything.

They turned up a flight of steps and walked to the top where they could see a vista across the river.

'Wow, that's quite a view! Mel exclaimed.

'Impressive, isn't it?'

'So it goes from here to that landing stage on The Wirral over there?'

'Yup.'

'Can you get vehicular access from over there?'

'Unfortunately, the road on top of the barrage will only take one-way traffic. Emergency vehicles only. No, we'll have to build a new roundabout and bring in a new access road from the A561 on this side, at our cost. Worth it though, as it will be only five minutes' drive to the airport and ten to the new bridge and the motorway system.'

She nodded. 'Very good. So will this barrage happen? So far as I can see it's vital to the overall development site.'

Puller laughed. 'Don't worry about that. I've got connections right across this city. I'm a local lad, and I'm well in with the MP, James Whitaker.'

She gave it a few seconds before she replied. 'You know, I think I could be onto something here, Mr Puller.'

'Call me Johnny.'

*

On the way back, Mel sensed that Puller was wrestling with the temptation to stroke her thigh, which, however much she squirmed and tried to pull her skirt down, was showing way too much flesh. Presumably these Porsche sports cars were specifically designed so that the skirt of a lady passenger would ride up the thigh. But, clearly, this could be a big commercial break and he couldn't risk lousing it up.

'Were you the same Johnny Puller who played in Creatures of Darkness with Oliver Gladwyn?'

'The very same one. Me and Oliver go way back.'

'Creatures of Darkness. Isn't that from a Roy Harper song?'

'Sure is. He was pals with Robert Plant and Jimmy Page; that's where we got the name.'

'There's a video on You Tube of you playing in Manchester with Led Zepp. You were good.'

Puller laughed and drummed his fingers on the dashboard as he drove. 'You certainly don't look old enough to have been at the original gig, baby. Remember the encore when we played with Zepp?'

'Well a whole lotta love!' they sang together.

That was lucky. It was the only Led Zeppelin number she knew.

CHAPTER TWENTY THREE

Jack upset himself before going to bed with his discovery that Leora Dana wasn't as strait-laced as she seemed in *3.10 to Yuma*, and now he couldn't sleep. In that film she was playing a part, obviously. But you tended to identify the actor or actress with the part you liked best. Like Felicity Farr who played the tarty barmaid in the film was probably prudish in real life. He'd googled Leora Dara to find out more about her and come up with an image that shocked him to the core. In place of neat black hair, golden locks flowed right down her back. She wore a tight t-shirt and shorts and sat on Cary Grant's lap in a way that implied that they were more than friends.

Jack couldn't remember if Grant was gay like Rock Hudson. He probably swung both ways like most movie stars of the time. And with Leora Dana in your lap, in a tight t-shirt and shorts you would just have to swing that way.

Now what was that name? He drummed his fingers on the desk and stared at the computer screen. He was tired, ready for bed, but there was one thing he had to check: *Ged Gibson, Solihull.* He googled it, but there were several of them. How could there be more than one Ged Gibson in such a little place as Solihull?

Try a different tack. He opened Facebook and entered *Ged Gibson, Solihull* into the search engine. Then he remembered. Gerard David Gibson. He added the second forename. One result. This guy didn't look like a dangerous psychopath in his photo—bearded, smiling, seaside location, sitting on a rock with the tide coming in, wearing T-shirt, shorts and sandals. Jack scrolled down the Facebook posts and stopped.

Hospital today. Arm still hurting.

Selfie in wheelchair. Several comments. One read: *That's terrible, Ged. Wasn't she held to account?* Ged replied: *My word against hers. Played the tearful abused wife. Jury swallowed it hook, line and sinker. She beat me to within an inch of my life. Put me in a wheelchair and gets away with it.* Several furious-looking faces were attached to the post.

Jack sat looking at the screen for a minute or so, then closed down Facebook. Time to go for a walk and think things through.

Outside, the mist hung low over the water, and he couldn't see the surface of the river, but he was aware of its presence—a low, rumbling hiss. Or was it a low, hissing rumble? He sensed that the river level was high, fed by recent rain in the hills. The light from the streetlamps off to one side was diffuse and pale yellow in the mist, giving everything the feel of being unreal. Another white night.

He was so deep in thought that he almost walked into the railings by the river. He paused for a moment to catch his bearings.

He hadn't been able to sleep. Again. Even though he'd made a vegetable curry using natural ingredients. He'd bought new potatoes, carrots and a cauliflower from the Tesco Express. He'd even thrown in a piece of root ginger and grated it in along with the turmeric and curry powder. And he'd only had one glass of red wine.

But the dreams were becoming stronger. Not so much hallucinatory now, but as real as something happening during the day, complete with sounds and smells. He had to try really hard to rise up to consciousness, as if some powerful animal had grabbed him and was trying to hold him down. He'd have to get help. But how? Ring up the therapist? Or just turn up on her doorstop?

He couldn't go back to the therapist. The original dream had been explained. The tortured person represented his guilt at his selfish lifestyle— particularly where women were concerned—and his resultant depression. The tree bathed in light represented a goal in life, one of wholeness and therefore happiness. But this last dream developed the theme of guilt, as if his unconscious was saying, 'Hang on, mate, I'm not finished with you just yet'. The tortured girl represented the girl who'd supposedly committed suicide. But then how could Jack be blamed for that? Maybe he had to sort out what had happened with the girl so she could rest easy in her grave. She was a Liverpool tart not worth a second thought, or so the forces who'd covered up her death seemed to be saying. No, he had to clear this up himself.

And now wasn't the best time to be having sleep problems that were causing him to be exhausted during the day. Mel had done a brilliant job on Johnny Puller. They now had a thick dossier that could put him behind bars. The problem was that that was not their brief. They were supposed to discretely investigate the link between Puller and Oliver Gladwyn and, in particular, the hold Puller had over Gladwyn. The murder of the informant who'd threatened their drugs business was one area for research. Jack was sure this was the key that would lead back to the truth behind Helen's disappearance. It might even lead to the truth behind Freddie's hatred for the Gladwyns. And then to Freddie. This hatred for the Gladwyns seemed to arise from a deeper source than historical wrongs. Trouble was, the murder had taken place in Australia and had been written off by the Aussie cops as an accidental drowning/shark attack. Jack had no links or contacts there, and there was no way he could investigate something like that from scratch.

He stood up from where he'd been leaning on the railings and started back to the flat. A figure loomed out of the mist; Jack nodded, and half mumbled a greeting, but the figure walked on without appearing to notice him.

A sound came from behind him. He half turned, but a terrific force hit him hard in the back, knocking all the breath from his body and sending him twisting against the railing.

'You should've kept out your nose out of Johnny Puller's affairs, knobhead,' hissed a voice in Jack's ear. Then strong arms lifted him and heaved him over the railing.

Jack seemed to be in the air for a long time, then he was in the river. The cold caused him to suck in air, but his mouth filled with water, and a terrible pain in his chest caused him to cough and splutter as he automatically kicked his arms and legs to fight his way to the surface. He sucked in great gasps. He was floating. Must be his clothes. They'd waterlog soon and drag him down. He saw yellow light not far away and kicked out as hard as he could towards it.

CHAPTER TWENTY FOUR

Dokka liked real ale. Dizzy Blonde especially, with its light hoppy taste. Though, when you came down to it, London Pride couldn't be beaten, with its rich fruitiness. This pub always had both beers on tap, and it was a great place to work on his laptop, nice and cool compared to the heat outside—just so long as you avoided the weekend when it was rammed with noisy, drunken young people. England might have the best beer and the best gentlemen, but it also had the worst hooligans and football fans. And, of course, it also had the worst government, one that oppressed and murdered Muslims worldwide.

Only one person sat at the bar, a man perched on a stool, razzled and old, but always nattily dressed; this time he wore a grey sports jacket, dark trousers and brown brogues. Plain clothes? Dokka always kept a careful watch out for anything new or untoward. No, this man was often in here. Local. Always spouting off about something in a loud voice.

The barman was down in the cellar, and the man was watching the racing on the telly. Dokka referred to him mentally as the 'old git'.

Now a lot of people might wonder why a man of his religion drank alcohol, but Dokka came from a suburb of Grozny where many enjoyed an occasional drink. Women didn't wear the veil or the burka, just a headscarf. And, of course, it was the perfect camouflage. Dokka was fair haired and skinned and spoke good English.

To anyone who asked, he was Romanian, a student working at his laptop on his coursework in Media Studies for his last year at John Moores University. If he was ever picked up and questioned, he had no need to lie. That was the principle; keep the need to lie as small as possible.

The idea of interrogation didn't bother him. After the horrors of Alkhan-Kala he knew he could stand almost anything. The road of blood and flesh. The Russians had lured them into a minefield as they'd retreated from Grozny. Young fighters had run ahead to clear a path and become martyrs. Many fighters lost legs, so many that they couldn't get all the casualties out. Some had to hop or run on bleeding stumps. Shrapnel had hit Dokka in the back and both legs. The piece in his back chopped up one of his kidneys. He'd never be a donor, though it didn't affect day-to-day life. He was as fit as a butcher's dog—apart from the legs, of course.

He took a sip of beer—glorious!—and went back to work researching the Jewish Nakam—his idea and one he was proud of. It was important in any conflict to get into the mind of the enemy and learn lessons that could be turned against them. Although he hated the Jews, he respected them. He'd carefully read up on the subject. A wise soldier knows his enemy so he can learn from his strengths and realistically assesses his weaknesses.

In 1948 they'd defeated several better-equipped Arab armies with militias armed with rifles, homemade Molotov cocktails, and whatever else they could beg, steal or borrow to use against Russian-supplied tanks, artillery and bombers. Dokka loved the account on the internet about how the Israelis had attacked Cairo with B17 Flying Fortresses bought as army surplus from the U.S., escorted by Czech-built Me109s. They'd been intercepted by Egyptian Spitfires supplied by the British. Amazing, like a scene from a Woody Allen film. And in 1967 the Israelis had carried out pre-emptive air strikes that destroyed the Arab air forces, giving them air supremacy and victory in six days.

The Jews certainly knew how to make war. It was like you might despise the S.S. but respect their ability to fight. He found it fascinating. After the holocaust in 1945, the Jewish survivors had set up a group called the Nokmim—meaning avengers—to punish the Germans. They poisoned several thousand S.S. prisoners by spreading arsenic on their bread.

Dokka loved this idea of poisoning the bread—'Enjoy your sandwich, asshole!' But he was more interested in the Jewish plan to poison the water supply of five German cities. They'd worked everything out and placed workers inside the cities' water filtration plants, but the British had arrested the operative carrying the poison from Israel to Germany. It was suspected that the man had been betrayed by his own side—a faction of which wanted to keep Israel's hands clean in the fight for nationhood.

Well, that wouldn't happen here. Dokka's side had learned their lessons. He was one of the few who knew the details of the plan. Things had changed since the 1940s, and with the War on Terror, the authorities kept a much more careful watch on their water supplies, using door keyboards and CCTV. Dokka himself would never get in. Had to be an inside job. You needed a carefully worked out plan with only one person in the key position. Him, Dokka. He was the minder.

And he'd worked out a fool-proof method of delivering the poison into the water supply. Tests had shown that arsenic would dissolve in mortar additive so that it was still potent but impossible to detect without taking samples and testing them in a fully equipped chemistry laboratory. All the city's water passed through the filtration plant where Alan was employed on the bricklaying training scheme. And what could be more innocuous than mortar additive to make the bricks get laid more easily? One five-litre plastic jerry can was all it took. Easily moveable by van.

Alan had copied the keys for one of the trainers' vans—a distinctive-looking, ex-post office vehicle with faded red paint and the letters 'GPO' just discernible on the side. The owner was a moron who did foreigners across the city using materials from the scheme. Alan had noted the kind of tub the mortar additive was kept in, and Dokka had bought the same one from Wickes. The arsenic had been delivered to his house in an innocuous-looking blue tub. He'd emptied the one from Wickes, filled it with the poison and used the keys to switch the tubs in the van parked outside the trainer's house.

Pick a quiet time, make a quick call on Alan's mobile with the code word, and Alan would get the tub out of the van and deliver it to half-a-million consumers via a hatch used to put fluoride or chlorine salts into the water supply.

He felt a flush of pride. Though his very existence was a secret now, in the future he would be lauded in school textbooks as a hero.

Yes, things were going well. As a treat to himself, he'd watch *The Manchurian Candidate* again when he got back to the flat. The 1957 original, of course, not some stupid remake. How he loved that film. Lawrence Harvey, Frank Sinatra and Angela

Lansbury. He'd read that, in the original book, the Harvey and Lansbury characters had sex before the final scene, but this had been cut from the screenplay because of the incest taboo and replaced with just a chaste little kiss.

He'd tried to read the book but had thrown it down at a third of the way through. It was a mishmash with no narrative thrust. See? He'd learned something on his college course. The film was much better in his opinion. Take the scene where the senator, asked to say how many communists there were in the US State department, gazes around in confusion before he eyes land on a tin of Heinz baked beans, then he says, '57!'

Sheer brilliance. The film was where they'd got the idea, of course. In return for the tactical nuclear weapon stolen from the Russian arms depot, the North Koreans had given them full use of their brainwashing unit, which they'd kept going since the Korean War—kept it ticking over processing kidnapped South Koreans. Fair swop.

He closed down the internet page, went into Word and selected '*The Paranoia Trilogy* of Alan Pakula' file—his dissertation topic for his degree in media studies at John Moores. *Klute, The Parallax View* and *All the President's Men.* He never tired of watching the films. He also regularly watched *The Manchurian Candidate* and *Chinatown,* but he had to concentrate on these three if he was to get the dissertation in on time and get his degree. And then?

He'd go home and start writing scripts, maybe even do some directing. The film industry in Chechnya was in its early days, and there was scope for a young man with bright ideas. His legs hurt again, and he had to squirm round to get into a more comfortable sitting position. He started to write:

> *The three films cover the years between the Kennedy assassination and the Nixon resignation: a time of paranoid unease in the USA, heightened by the ever-increasing horrors of Vietnam shown on the TV every night. And if you were a young man at this time, you had some skin in the game. You might be called up, handed a rifle and thrust into the jungle to fight the Cong yourself. Unless you had a rich daddy, of course.*

He was going like a train.

> *It is this feeling of increasing paranoid unease that typifies these films and much of this is down to the camera work. Telling scenes are filmed elliptically, either through glass windowpanes, gauze curtains or at a distance, which imparts an air of conspiracy and a sense of powerlessness on the part of the viewer. As you watch you get the feeling that this is really happening, and you are just observing it, but you are unable to intervene.*

Dokka was only too aware personally of this feeling of paranoid unease: going through airport customs, trying to remain cool knowing that someone might be watching for signs of nervousness; walking down the street, wondering if he was being followed.

The camerawork is brilliant: objects disappear as if by magic; a massive slab of glass disgorges tiny figures; the use of silence when characters stare into space. In The Parallax View, *at the end, the protagonist rushes from darkness toward the light of an open doorway but is gunned down before he can make it.*

Dokka thought for a moment. He was on a roll. This was good. He continued typing.

It is easy to confuse this feeling of paranoia with popularly believed conspiracy theories of the time—the Kennedy assassination, the moon landing. The key thing is not that the government might want to assassinate a president or fabricate a moon landing, but the problem is that too many people, thousands, would have had to be involved in such a conspiracy. So many that, over time, it would inevitably get out. Human nature.

His legs were stiff, and he had to move yet again. He didn't want to take more painkillers just yet.

Conspiracy is the recurring theme in the three films. In The Parallax View *it is political assassination. In* Klute *it is the escape from justice of a politically powerful killer—much like Noah Cross in Chinatown. In* All the President's Men *it is the covering up of underhand tactics by the most powerful person in the world: the American president. In* The Manchurian Candidate *it is a plot by enemies of the USA to take control of that country.*

Perhaps, *the pinnacle—if you can call it that—in this conspiracy theory nightmare, the point of maximum chill factor when your body, its hairs, its skin, its heartbeat, reacts out of your conscious control, is in the scene in* All The President's Men *when Deep Throat informs the two journalists that their lives are in danger. What? In America? Democratic America? Land of the Free?*

Dokka reflected. His organisation didn't want to take control of the USA and the West; they wanted to destroy the whole stinking lot of them. He had cramp in his legs now, and he had to sit bolt upright with the pain. The whole stinking, corrupt lot of them. He couldn't say that in this dissertation, obviously, but his real experience of paranoia, a feeling of unease and conspiracy, gave him a key insight. A thought struck him: the battle of Chechnya against the power of the Russian empire. Now that might be a fertile background for a screenplay.

*

The old git at the bar sidled over. 'The sooner we leave this European Union the better,' he said, as if he were continuing a conversation. 'All these immigrants coming in and taking our jobs!'

Dokka couldn't think of anything to say, so he just grinned at the man.

The old git grinned back. 'No offence, mate. I don't mean people like you. Apologies. You're from Poland, aren't you?'

'Romania.'

'Oh, so you're not a plumber?'

'No, I'm a student. Media Studies.'

'Skilled? I've got nothing against skilled people. They help the economy, don't they? No, it's unskilled and semi-skilled people coming in for lower pay and taking our jobs.' He leaned over to look at the screen.

Dokka quickly closed it down. Had he seen his name? It was in the top right-hand corner of the page of his dissertation. He smiled.

'The man smiled back. 'So whereabouts in Romania are you from?' he said.

'Sofia.' Dokka finished off his beer and snapped the laptop shut. 'Got to be going.'

It was a shame he'd have to change the pub in which to meet Alan. The beer in here was so good.

CHAPTER TWENTY FIVE

First Mel needed to find out if the surveillance debacle had blown her cover. She typed in *Hi, Jane, not heard from you for a while. Been caught up with single mom stuff. How's it going?* After a couple of minutes, a reply came back. *No problems! Tell me about the single mom stuff – it's mad in this house at the moment. Bath time – will catch up with you later. Nice to hear from you!*

Mel checked the posts on Facebook. Nothing about the barrage—a lot about an upcoming demo against fracking near Southport. She followed the debate for a while: pollution of groundwater; earthquakes—that was a bit worrying—continuation of dependence on fossil fuels. Nearly all the posts were vehemently opposed, but one called Joe—an old gent by the look of his picture—pointed out that the people at these demos were all NIMBYs, that the latest demo on the telly was down south in Tory-voting Surrey, and they wouldn't be bothered if it was somewhere up north.

, replied Jane, *thank you for that, Joe; we always welcome a dissenting voice. But I don't live anywhere near the site so I can hardly be called a NIMBY.*

Mel expected Joe to reply with something to the effect that she was a mad anarchist who would be against fracking wherever it was proposed, but no, the old duffer missed the opportunity. Maybe playing along with his role as the tolerated, polite dissenting voice. Any nastiness or vitriol and he'd have been shunted off the group sharpish.

Mel felt tired. It was late in the evening, and she was fed up with making things up on Facebook. Harriet had fallen asleep at last, and it was time for a big gin and tonic. She wasn't posting all lies since many of the views she expressed were actually her own. The golden rule was not to lie but to bend the truth. She did feel unhappy with the government's lack of focus on climate change. She wouldn't go so far as to propose the dragging of the said politicians out of their comfortable offices and stringing them up from the nearest lamppost as some wanted, but she could sympathise. If you were totally against something and pretending otherwise, it showed.

And too many of her new anarchist friends on Facebook had a pie-in-the-sky, looking-through-rose-tinted-spectacles attitude to the chances of their local experiments succeeding when pitted against the power of the modern industrial state. Too much mutual patting on the back, getting up each other's arseholes—like when middle-aged female friends complimented each other's posted photos, calling them 'Drop dead gorgeous', when it was patently obvious that the photo showed a plain, fat, middle-aged woman. She wasn't far off being a plain, fat, middle-aged women herself, but what was the point in deluding yourself? Give support and build confidence, yes, but not at the expense of obvious truth.

She turned from the laptop and gripped the edge of the table.

'Stop this!' she shouted out loud. 'Stop this now, Melanie Gibson! This is typical female cattiness. The worst kind of misogyny, inflicted by female on female.'

She closed down her laptop, then, on a whim, started it up again and googled *Jack Gordon*. She was amazed at the results. Hundreds of posts came up, many stemming from a website called *Jansfriends*. She clicked on it. The site had been set up by the friends—all female it looked like—of a lady called Jan Gordon. They accused Jack of abandoning her and her child and avoiding paying maintenance. Apparently, he'd moved house many times to avoid his pursuers from the Child Maintenance Agency, though they'd recently tracked him down to a housing scheme on the Liverpool docks—details to follow.

Mel read through the site, carefully. The images of the women were remarkably similar to the images of her new Facebook friends. She checked some of the names. No, that would've been too much of a coincidence. Then she came to a bit that made her stop and stare: accusations about not only abandonment and evasion of his parental responsibilities but also violence against his former wife—who, it seemed, had kept the name. But Jack had told Mel that the wife was denying access to the kid, yet was happy to take the money every month. Mel had almost burst into tears herself when he'd told her the story. Or maybe that was another wife?

It was possible, of course, that all this stuff about Jack was faked or lies. 'Heaven hath no fury as love to hatred turned.' You couldn't believe anything you read on the internet without carefully checking its veracity. She was living proof of that. Though there seemed to be a lot of them for it to be a put-up job to dig some gold. Again, they might feed off each other's stories.

She closed down the laptop and leaned back in her chair. The house was quiet. Harriet was asleep for once.

She'd have to take this bullying thing seriously—go in and see the form teacher, the head teacher if needs be. Harriet might be exaggerating, but Mel didn't think so. It was a problem of low self-esteem and seeking attention. The two worked off each other. Trouble was, if she was like this at eight, what would she be like at thirteen? Mel shuddered at the memory of how awkward and rebellious she'd been at thirteen. And there was no father to help.

And not much prospect of getting one. Not even a partner at the moment. Unless ... Johnny Puller. Very attractive. But that number plate *PULL 1*. Do me a favour! And he was a subject of surveillance—probably a gangster, possibly a murderer. Be professional. Get friendly but not too friendly. She'd ring the school the first chance she got.

But how to play Jack when she met him in the morning? They'd need to compare notes after their meetings with Gladwyn and Puller. She'd have to play it straight. No mention of this little bit of gossip that she'd culled from the internet.

She'd always taken Jack Gordon as a pretty straight guy. Okay, there was all that Flash Gordon and Jumping Jack Flash stuff, but he'd given her a job in her hour of need and had been the total gentleman when she rebuffed his advances. But if even a small percentage of what they were saying on the website was true, then he was just another bullshit merchant.

She got up and went downstairs to make a cup of tea, standing by the kettle as it warmed up. A scuffing sound came from outside in the garden, like something rubbing on wood. A fox? She'd seen one walking down the middle of the road outside the house in broad daylight. At first, she'd thought it was a little dog that had escaped from someone's garden, but this estate was definitely not one where stray dogs roamed the streets. She switched off the kettle, turned off the light and took the rechargeable light that she kept hanging by the back door. Outside the sky was cloudy and everything was quiet. A dog barked somewhere then abruptly stopped. She waited for her eyes to get used to the darkness, then edged down the path towards the back fence.

She could hear something: breathing; too loud for an animal. She switched on the light and shone it towards the rear boundary. A large shape perched on top of the wooden fence.

'What the fuck!' came a low voice.

Mel stepped forward, keeping the light on the shape. Now she could see that it was a man, a big man with a big head, perched on the top of the fence and teetering forwards then back, out of balance.

She needed a weapon. She should've got a carving knife or a pair of scissors from the kitchen drawer like the women in the movies who are threatened in their house by an intruder.

With a loud ripping sound, the section of fence the intruder sat on collapsed, flinging him face forwards onto the ground.

Mel stepped back and stumbled on something. She shone the light at it. A log about two feet long and four inches thick. Perfect.

Holding the light on the intruder, who'd got onto his knees and was moaning in pain, she picked up the log, ran forward and whacked him hard across the shoulders. He cried out and crouched down with his hands over his head. She hit him as hard as she could on the arms then, as he tried to crawl away, hit him on the back of the head. He collapsed face forward onto the ground with a grunt, out cold. With some difficulty she managed to get his small rucksack off him and upend the contents onto the ground. Her light showed plastic ties, a rubber cosh, thin plastic gloves, a torch and a length of rope—a kidnapping kit.

She looked up. The man was crawling away. He managed to get to his feet and stumble over a low fence into next door's garden. The lights came on in the next door's house, and a door opened, sending a shaft of light that caught the intruder like a rabbit in a headlight. A big man with a big head, dressed in black, with a balaclava on his head.

'Who's there?' came an angry voice.

The intruder ran past the angry neighbour and along the drive at the side of the house. He must've been wearing soft-soled shoes, for his footsteps soon receded into the night.

CHAPTER TWENTY SIX

'Jack! Jack! Help me!'

The voice sounded close in the water. Female. There it was again. Shouldn't it be muffled in the water? How did it sound so clear in water that was like thick brown soup? Not cold. Can't see a thing. Rely on hearing like a whale or a dolphin. He tried to swim towards the voice, but he never seemed to get any closer.

Then something wrapped around his head, his throat, strangling him. A rope? He tried to get his fingers into it so he could breathe, but it tightened on his fingers, cutting into them. He clawed them loose, but the coarse fibres of the rope cut into the flesh of his throat. He gasped and kicked but was gradually dragged upwards where he surfaced into intense yellow light, gasping for breath.

'Hold on there, mate!' came a voice from above.

'Shit, it's round his neck!' Another voice. 'We'll strangle the poor twat.'

'Pull him towards the steps. I'll go down and release him.'

The rope pulled Jack—choking, gasping and struggling—along in the water. He felt something under his feet and crawled out onto steps. Hands pulled the rope from his neck. He lay there, gasping.

A face appeared, its features clear in the intense light: a big nose, spiky hair. Barry Chuckle? Rod Stewart? No, it was Harry, the security man.

'Jack? I thought it was you. Come on, mate. There's everything to live for. It's not as bad as it seems!'

'What?' Jack spluttered. 'I was pushed.'

'I thought I heard someone running away. Who was it?'

'I dunno. A mugger?'

Jack had a good idea who the attacker was. It was no mugger. If you wanted someone's wallet, you didn't push them in the river. Maybe when you'd got it you would. No, this was attempted murder.

'Whoever it was, they knew their stuff,' Harry said. 'There's nothing on CCTV. It's possible to avoid the camera sweeps, but you've got to be quick and know what you're doing.' He took Jack by the arm. 'Come on, mate, let's get you up to your flat.'

Harry helped him walk. Jack's shoes squelched loudly, and he felt cold now. The other rescuer had disappeared into the night.

In the flat, Jack put the biggest towel he could find around himself, and Harry made him a mug of tea, which Jack gratefully accepted.

Harry sat down opposite him and stared at Jack earnestly. 'Will you be all right?' Harry's face shone in the bright light, making his conk seem even bigger than usual. 'You don't want me to call the police?'

Jack shook his head.

'Look, mate,' Harry continued. 'I don't know who's got it in for you, but this is getting serious. Is it someone you owe money to? Though I suppose it would defeat the object, pushing you in the river. You were a copper, weren't you? Maybe a villain with a score to settle?' He grinned. 'Someone whose wife you've been shagging?'

Jack laughed. 'Something like that,' he said.

Harry turned to go and paused. 'Look mate, if you got any problems just share them.'

Jack stopped himself from making an angry retort. The guy had saved his life, after all. 'Like I said,' Jack said calmly. 'I was pushed. I've got no problems big enough to make me jump in the river.'

Harry shrugged. 'Okay. If you need anything, you know where I am.'

Once he was alone, Jack ran a bath and lowered himself into the warm water. Luxury. He lay with his head against the back of the bath, just letting the warmth seep through his body. An image crept into his mind: Leora Dana on Cary Grant's knee. Oh my, oh my.

*

The phone went off.

Fuck! He'd fallen asleep in the bath. The water was freezing. Early morning light peeped through the join in the curtains.

He sat up, reached for a towel, then headed for the phone, his wet feet making little farting noises on the wood-panelled floor as he walked.

'Jack? It's Sarah. Sarah Gladwyn. We've been attacked again. This time at the big house. Jack, we need your help!'

CHAPTER TWENTY SEVEN

Even at nine thirty, well after the morning rush hour, the A55 was busy. The car's air con was acting up again, so Jack had to have the widows open, but that meant the car filled with heat and fumes, and he couldn't hear the music properly. At the moment another of his favourites from the eighties played. He tapped his fingers on the steering wheel in time to the music.

Of course, the new bridge meant that you cruised out of Liverpool much quicker than in the old days, sweeping past Helsby Hill on the left and the new wind turbines with their blades turning slowly on the right, then past the chimneys of the chemical works smoking and burning. But coming past Queensferry, the traffic slowed to walking pace, not because of any accident or roadworks, just the sheer amount of traffic.

He checked his face in the mirror. The wound had started to heal, but he'd developed a huge bruise that took in not only his nose but also part of each cheek. It was a strange mix of colours: mauves, ochres and yellows with the tracks of blood vessels— a sight to behold. It looked like the William Morris wallpaper his mother had been so fond of.

It was a relief to pull off onto the B-road, which wound its way through the foothills of Snowdonia, with clean air cool on his face.

'Your destination is on the right,' said the smooth and classy sounding lady on the satnav. Jack often wondered what she was like in real life— probably an old crone.

The Gladwyn house had an impressive entrance with big gateposts then an avenue of ancient beech trees. He felt a little disappointed when he reached the house itself. Though called 'Gladwyn Castle' on the maps, it was actually just a big detached Victorian house. Then he remembered that the actual castle had been left to the National Trust when old man Gladwyn died. He caught a glimpse of it up on the hillside through the trees. It was only a mock castle anyway—he'd googled it—built in 1820 with the profits from slate mining and slave and sugar trading.

A gardener working on a flower bed looked up as Jack pulled onto the gravel drive in front of the house. A big fellow, maybe in his fifties, he had a thinning blonde mop which might once have been a glorious pompadour. He turned away at Jack's nod.

Nothing like a friendly welcome.

The house was one of those exotic Victorian Gothic confections with fancy gables and bargeboards, and ornate iron balustrades under the curved windows. The only concession to the local area was the use of grey slate blocks in the walls and blue slates in the construction of the roof. Jack quite liked the style. It reminded him of his own family house in Liverpool—though it was nowhere near as big as this one.

The sky was overcast, and a cool breeze played across the patio. Sarah came down the steps to greet him. She looked fabulous in fawn slacks and white shirt—a real country lady.

'So you found us okay?' She peered at his face. Her eyes looked a deeper shade of green than he remembered. 'Your nose seems to be healing up nicely.'

'It still hurts. My professional pride that is. You must have thought, what a wally.' He paused. 'Mr Gladwyn's not here?'

'No, he's got important business in Liverpool.'

Jack breathed a sigh of relief. If Oliver Gladwyn had been around, he'd no doubt have wondered why a supposed *Guardian* reporter was also acting as a private eye. 'So what's the latest?' he said. 'Is it Freddie the Ferret and his merry band?'

'Come on; I'll show you.' She put on a fawn cardigan which had been draped over a chair and guided him towards the back of the house where a large patio paved in huge slate slabs looked out over oak woods, low hills and the odd green field to Snowdonia.

Jack tried to remember from his youth when his family spent holidays camping and mountain walking here. Was that Snowdon? The three pointed one must be Tryfan. Off to one side, he glimpsed the sea beyond the mountains. 'That's some view,' he said, stopping to take it in.

'Nice, isn't it?'

'So I take it this isn't the actual Gladwyn castle.'

She laughed. 'No, that was too expensive to run. My father gave it to the nation before my time. This place is big enough as it is. What do you do with twenty bedrooms when you only need half a dozen?' She pointed. 'There it is.'

A message written in red letters about six inches high scrawled across the glass of a large window in a lean-to conservatory: *Thought we'd forgotten about you? Don't worry Gladwyn trash your come-uppance is at hand.*

'When was this done?'

'It must have been last night. No one heard anything.'

Jack examined it. 'At least it's not a bomb. Have you told the police?'

'No. They're not much use.'

'Hmmm.' The local plods should really be informed, but there was no real damage. He poked with a fingernail and managed to lift off a flake of paint. 'It's ordinary gloss paint,' he said. 'It'll come off with a bit of white spirit. They obviously just wanted to send the message, not cause vandalism. Don't clean it off yet. I'll take some photos. Who lives here at the moment?'

'Just the maid and the gardener. They have rooms on the top floor.'

'Kids?'

'At school.' She looked at him and added, 'Look, would you like some tea? It's a bit of a drive from Liverpool.'

'I'll just have a look around the grounds.'

'You'll need walking boots. The perimeter is about two miles round.'

'Wall?'

'About eight feet high. Easily climbable. Not really a barrier.'

'Sounds like a security nightmare. Any cameras? Alarms?'

'No. It's a very secluded spot.'

He turned to her and tried to look stern. 'Mrs Gladwyn, these people torched your husband's car. The same gang is suspected of burning down a police laboratory; for all they knew some plod might've been working late. It could well have been arson and murder. I strongly suggest that I do a quick survey and get one of our trusted contractors to prepare a detailed security plan.'

A maid appeared with a tray of tea things, and they moved to the patio and sat at an ornate, black-metal table and chairs. Jack got the strange feeling that they were old friends having a good natter over a cup of tea.

'Were you brought up here?' he said. 'Nice playground.'

She laughed. 'All two hundred acres. Yes, me and Helen roamed across this place when we were young.' She laughed at his quizzical expression. 'I should have said Helen and I, of course; I did go to a very expensive school. My old English teacher wouldn't have been amused.' She dabbed her eyes with a tissue from the cuff of her cardigan. 'We were very close. You can get down to the beach, you know. It's a private beach.' She stood up. 'Come and have a look.'

He followed her across the lawn and then to the side of the house through trees to a gravel footpath which led into a wood. They walked side by side as if they were a happy couple who'd been together for years. She led him to a rock outcrop. They scrambled up to see a view out over a ravine with woods falling steeply to the sea and a deserted beach. Gulls and oystercatchers called mournfully down below. Sunlight glinted off a choppy sea.

'Anglesey's not far away,' she said. 'Just the other side of those woods.'

He stretched to look and she laughed.

'You can't see it,' she said. 'We used to walk along the beach to the village. It wasn't quite so touristy then. We had a privileged upbringing, of course, but we loved the wildness of it. We made dens. Helen fell out of a tree once. Broke her wrist.' She paused and sat on a boulder. He sat on another one opposite her. 'Look, Mr Gordon,' she said. 'Can I tell you something? In confidence?'

'Of course.'

'I still hope against hope that my sister is alive.' She dabbed at her eyes with the tissue. 'She was vivacious. Everyone said so. She was more outgoing than me …'

He laughed.

'No, I was always the quiet one,' she continued. 'She had her whole life ahead of her. About to go to university. She was the last person in this world to commit suicide. Will you help me find her?'

He couldn't think of a reply. 'It's been a long time …'

'No, I've got this feeling, Mr Gordon. She's alive. I know it.'

He didn't reply.

'Look,' she said, her voice lower now. 'I don't like Johnny Puller. He has some kind of hold over my husband. I know Oliver's got a colourful past, but Puller's got something on him. Otherwise Oliver wouldn't have made him a partner just like that, Mr Gordon.'

'What's with the Mr Gordon?' he said. 'Call me Jack.'

'No, I prefer to keep this on a professional footing. Mr Gordon, will you do what you can to find Helen and to find out what this hold is that he has over Oliver?'

*

Jack bombed down the A55 at ninety miles an hour. Fuck the speed traps; he needed to get back. His mobile rang.

'Jack? Jack are you there?' His dad sounded breathless and very excited. 'I've caught one trying to break in. He's locked in the cellar.'

CHAPTER TWENTY EIGHT

Jack's dad met him on the doorstep, a baseball bat in one hand and his big service revolver, illegally retained from National Service, in the other.

'He's in the cellar!' he said, intense excitement in his voice. 'Don't worry, it's a good sturdy lock in a heavy door. There's no way he's going anywhere.'

'Who is it? Did you get a look at him?'

'I think it's one of those hooligans from the other day in the pub.'

'Okay, let me take a look around. You go and make a cup of tea, Dad. Just relax. I'll sort it out. Here, let me take those.' Jack took the bat and the revolver off his dad and put the bat behind the front door. Once his dad had gone to make some tea, Jack checked the revolver and discovered that it was fully loaded and dangerous. Good God! He put the safety on and hid it in the glove compartment of his car. Then he walked around the property.

The big Victorian house was becoming neglected. What had made it such a good playground when he was a kid—size, number of rooms where you could hide, overgrown grounds— now made it a nightmare to maintain. The window frames needed to be rubbed down and given a good coat of paint. The gutters had grass and little trees growing out of them. And from the rubbish strewn along the boundary with the property next door, it looked like the neighbours treated his dad's garden as a convenient rubbish dump.

He walked round the back to where stone steps led down to the cellar. Above the door at the bottom, a small window sat slightly ajar.

'I'm warning you knobheads!' came a muffled voice, the owner of which sounded rather pissed off. 'I'm sweating my cobs off in here, lar.' Pause. 'I've got a reputation round here for being a hard-case. Let me go now and I'll think about letting you off.'

Jack squinted through the window, but dust covered it and it was dark inside. 'Well, well,' he said. 'If it's not me old mate, Eddie Malone. I think you'd better be a bit more polite if you want to get out of there. What were you doing breaking into private property?'

Silence from inside.

Eventually a much calmer voice said, 'I know you Jack Gordon. Flash Gordon they call you, don't they? Ex copper. Think you're some kind of private eye, don't you? Knobhead.' Silence. 'And your stupid sidekick Melanie what's her name. The one who put my mate Gobby in hospital.'

'Couldn't have happened to a nicer feller,' Jack said. 'And he should've picked on someone his own size.'

Silence.

'Knobhead.'

'I could leave you there overnight. Should get nice and cold in there. Never mind the heat wave.'

'I'm just a hired help. The boss told us to help the hold outs—I mean owners—who won't accept the generous offer they've been made and move on.'

'This boss wouldn't be Johnny Puller, would it? And you wouldn't know anything about me being pushed in the river last night and left to drown.'

Silence.

'Look.' The voice was quieter now. 'Mr Puller doesn't like you nosing around in his affairs.'

'Affairs? 'You mean money laundering and other such activities? I'm not paid to look into that.'

'Knobhead!'

'Right, you're in for the night. No mod cons.'

'Come on, mate. Turn the light on. There's no toilet. What about food and water?'

'Light, food, water? Luxury. You'll be wanting a nice warm bed next.'

'Come on, mate. This is like *Breaking Bad*.'

'And look how that ended. Walter couldn't release the rival drug dealer on account of him being a violent thug who wouldn't keep his word not to harm him or his family. And when he tried to break free, Walter had to do him in. Dissolved him in acid.'

The silence lasted for several minutes.

'Okay, what do you want to know?'

'Why is Puller harassing my dad?'

'He needs all the property for this big development associated with the barrage. He can't afford any ransom strips.'

'Ransom strips?

'Yeah, where someone holds onto a small piece of land that's vital to a big development so they can ask what they like of the developer.'

'My dad's not like that. He just wants to be left alone.'

'Yeah, well, Johnny can't afford to slip up. The head honchos of the rough and tumble side of this operation are due out of the clink any day now, and they'll want a return on their investment.'

'You mean the money they provided to be laundered.'

'Ha, so you are paid to look into something. Knobhead!'

'Calm down, calm down!' Jack put on his best scouse accent.

'Don't tell me to calm down, knobhead. I hate that Harry Enfield.'

'Okay, Okay, so how come Gladwyn's made Puller his preferred partner?'

'I don't know.'

'Come on, give us a clue. Give us something to go on, and I'll get you a nice cold drink of water.'

Silence.

He's got something on him,' Malone said. 'Something from his past. I don't know what.'

CHAPTER TWENTY NINE

'Thump! Crump!'

The explosions were close by. He felt the vibrations rolling through his body. Sam was muttering something, but Alan couldn't make it out. Greyness everywhere: grey dust; eyes itching; lips stuck together.

Something popped nearby. The ammo for the machine gun! Got to get out. Sam in the way. Groaning. Moaning. He was in the burning Warrior. Couldn't make out what Sam was moaning. And then he was in the hospital, and the nurses were changing the dressing on the wound on his back. It was stuck on and they couldn't get it off.

'Ah!' he screamed.

The nurses laughed. 'We've got a right little soldier boy here!'

Alan woke up.

'Thump! Crump!'

In a brief interlude between explosions, he heard his mobile going off. Ignore it. He lay in bed. In his flat. It was hot in the small bedroom. He kept the windows shut to keep out any noise, but even sleeping with just the sheet on top meant that he sweated like a pig.

He reached for the glass on the table by the side of the bed. Empty. He reached for the vodka bottle. Empty, too. Then a lager can. All empty.

The explosions started again outside. He got up, went over to the window and pulled the curtains. Flash of dazzling lights. Fountain of sparks. Loud hissing. He stepped back and shielded his eyes with a hand.

Fireworks again! On a lunchtime! And it was nowhere near November the fifth. They came from the same garden of one of the sold-off Council houses that backed onto the housing association flats where Alan lived. A party was in full swing: loud music; smoke from a barbecue; shouts; cheers when a firework went off. They all seemed to end in the same frighteningly loud bang.

'Whump! Crump!'

It was no good calling the police. The housing association wouldn't do anything either. And the fucking social worker was useless—looked like Jeremy Corbyn, with white hair and beard. His idea of stopping anti-social behaviour would be to share a nice cup of tea and some digestive biscuits with the toe rags and then everything would continue as before.

It was no use going down and asking them nicely. They were a family of roughnecks. He'd tried that before and got a mouthful of filth for his troubles. And they didn't leave it there. They harassed you whenever you went outside, like at the local shops. Once, a thrown bottle had hit Alan on the back. They'd had a good laugh over that, but they wouldn't be laughing if Alan manged to get his hands on one of those heavy machine guns they had in a Warrior. Or, even better, the twenty-millimetre cannon that some models had—designed for destroying soft-skinned vehicles and enemy infantry. Alan had seen an Iraqi soldier cut right in two by one of them. That'd do the trick.

No, what was needed was some good old-fashioned justice. Vigilante justice.

CHAPTER THIRTY

They had the lights on in the council chamber even though bright sunlight shone outside, but to Mel it was still a gloomy place—more like a tomb than somewhere you might meet and converse, or maybe share a joke, with fellow human beings. Dark wood panelling everywhere and huge oil paintings—one particularly large one showed an unhappy looking Victorian alderman in long black robes. The only natural light came from windows high up on the wall. The electric lights were a joke—candles would've been better. At least it felt cooler than outside.

'Cheer up!' she felt like saying to the alderman in the painting. 'You control Liverpool, the main port of the British Empire at the height of its power. The world is your oyster.'

Gladwyn was just coming to the end of his presentation. The steering committee, made up mainly of local-government councillors and officers, was rapt, taking in every word. And so they should be, seeing as the greying hippy standing at the lectern was asking them to underwrite his barrage project to the tune of several-hundred-million pounds. Biggest ever infrastructure project in Merseyside, even bigger than the new bridge—and that had been totally funded via private investment.

'James?'

The chair, the leader of Wirral Council as it said on the sign in front of him, turned his head towards James Whitaker, M.P. for Liverpool South. All the leaders of the Merseyside local authorities were present. They seemed to be looking to him, James Whitaker, for direction.

'Thank you for that interesting presentation, Oliver.' Tall, dark and handsome, Whitaker was instantly recognisable from his many appearances on the box. Clearly destined for high office. Though Mel found something oily and unpleasant about him. 'Perhaps when electricity becomes as cheap as you say it will be, we can get some proper lighting in this chamber so we can keep a track of what's going on.'

No one laughed. They weren't that far up Whitaker's arse, and they'd let the world know it. No, it wasn't the time for political whims, favours and voting according to the slate. It was time for economic rigour and common sense.

'What impressed me with the presentation, Chair,' Whitaker continued, 'was the economic case. The tides are always with us, twice a day non-stop, every day. No clouds or windless periods. No poisonous waste left for future generations to dispose of. No dependence on the hurt feelings or otherwise of some Arab sheikh. No, once you put up the capital, it's constant energy for a hundred years. In fact, it's hard to think of a safer bet when it comes to underwriting investment. And Mr Gladwyn has made a pretty good stab at placating the fishermen and the bird watchers. I say go with it.'

'Just hold your horses there, Mr Whitaker.' Councillor Bingham, Chair of Liverpool Council's Economic Development and Planning Committee, looked like a bit of a leftie, a troublemaker. 'Could we just go back to your slide detailing the costs, Mr Gladwyn.'

Gladwyn did so. The slide showed a table comparing the Mersey project with the proposed Swansea barrage and the proposed Hinkley Point C nuclear power station.

'This figure of eighty pounds per megawatt hour,' continued Bingham, 'compared to Swansea at eight-nine ninety and Hinkley Point at ninety-two ninety-five; this is the figure to be guaranteed by the government and this committee?'

'That is correct, Councillor. That allows us to pay off the construction loan and make a profit.'

'And what if the price of oil, say, soars, and your income goes up, don't we get a share in those profits?'

'You do. Appendix three of the business plan and section four of the draft agreement make that clear.'

'Oh, I've not had time to read all the papers.' He shuffled his notes. 'But there's one more thing.'

'Yes?' Gladwyn was obviously making every effort to be patient.

'What about risk. What if a Boeing 747 crashes into it? Or terrorists blow it up with a bomb?'

'There would, of course, be the standard security measures to guard a key piece of this country's infrastructure. But, if the worst came to the worst, we would be covered by our insurance. Which I assure you, doesn't come cheap. Check out the figures in the cash flows in the appendix to the business plan.'

Gladwyn looked as if he were directly addressing the stern-looking alderman on the wall over the chair's shoulder, as if to say, 'Cheer up you old bugger. This is a safer bet than the canal system.' Providing the fucking thing didn't develop leaks. Mel wondered if they'd thought about that one.

Loud voices came from the corridor. The door crashed open and several middle-aged, thickset men in full black-rubber body waders—fishermen?—burst in carrying a large metal canister between them. They dropped it on its side; the lid flew off and water flooded across the floor with a large mass of squirming grey and silver creatures.

Fish? Mel stared. One skidded closer to her writhing like a snake. Eels.

'Ladies and gentlemen!' One of the men addressed the astounded people in the chamber, stunned into silence by the interruption. 'The numbers of eels in this country's waters have collapsed to one per cent of what they used to be. They've just started to recover in the Mersey after the recent clean-up, and you propose to build a barrage with a ladder for salmon and sea trout but not for eels!'

'Well, I think you need an eel ladder, Mr Gladwyn,' Whitaker said, his face deadpan.

Everyone in the chamber laughed, apart from Oliver Gladwyn who stood speechless.

'Meet that condition,' continued Whitaker, 'and you've got your approval.'

As he delivered these words, several security guards shepherded out the fishermen. One tried to catch an eel, but it squirmed out of his fingers and hit the floor with a loud slap.

CHAPTER THIRTY ONE

So what to do with the psychopathic thug in the basement? Jack pondered this while cleaning his dad's house. It wasn't so much dirty as dusty and neglected. He emptied the kitchen bin, washed up all the dirty plates in the sink and checked the fridge and the cupboards. Tea bags, sugar, a jar of strawberry jam, a tub of marge, a half-empty plastic bottle of milk and a couple of tins of beans. Not a vitamin to be seen. As bad as Roy. Jack would have to do some shopping and cook a meal. And do some for the thug in the cellar?

In the hallway he moved the piles of newspapers into the front room and threw out the rubbish. The papers had all to be kept, of course. His dad would go mental if Jack threw out a single page.

Malone would make all kinds of promises to be set free, then happily renege on each one. No, Jack needed some kind of hold over him. But what? He couldn't be imprisoned indefinitely. It was against the law for a start. And suppose his pals, like this Gobby, came looking for him? And he'd have to be fed and watered, provided with somewhere to sleep and somewhere to go to the toilet. In a prison you'd get light and reading materials. It was a nightmare.

Jack moved the last of the newspapers—all yellowing and brittle with age. The pile he was manhandling sent a cloud of dust into the air, making him sneeze. He staggered into the front room and set the pile down on one of the few remaining empty spaces on the floor.

The date on the top paper on a pile of *Liverpool Echos* read May 1998. When did Sally die? June of that year. Coincidence or what? More like synchronicity. Jack squatted beside the pile, shuffled through the papers and eventually found it: Wednesday June 14ᵗʰ, 1998; front page; photo of police divers in river; headline, *Tragedy of Local Girl.*

The picture of the girl, Sally Parker, reminded him of someone. He got out his mobile, searched for the Liverpool Registry Office, rang the number and gave them a cock and bull story about trying to trace a wayward sister. He got the answer: Sally Parker was the girl's married name; her maiden name was Sally Malone.

It was well into the afternoon by the time he got to West Derby. The last pub he tried, The Pied Piper, was the roughest one in the area—flat roof, tired décor. At this time of day, it was the haunt of elderly alkies—missing their front teeth and with a permanent pint of lager in one hand. Even though Roy had promised to go on the wagon, Jack was sure he'd be in a pub somewhere. And he was—sitting in the corner with his face in a copy of the *Daily Mail*.

He looked up, surprised, when Jack sat alongside him. 'What brings you here, chief?'

'Just checking something out. Remember Sally Parker, the tart who jumped in the river. 1998?'

'Yeh. Supposed to have jumped in the river. Pushed more likely.'

'What makes you say that? I thought it was us putting the pressure on her to grass.'

'More like she was under pressure not to grass on something else. Remember that kid who was crucified in Sefton Park, nailed to an oak tree with a sign pinned to his chest? *Grass* it said. She was a witness.'

Jack shook his head in exasperation. 'Why didn't you let on at the time?' he said.

'I was frightened, mate. You must've been the only copper in the squad who didn't know. Sally Parker was a witness to the crucifixion.' He took a gulp of lager. 'Puller and Tyrer were involved. Anyone who pried too deeply would've gone in the river too.'

Back at his dad's house, Jack found an old plastic chair amongst the rubbish in the garden. He parked it by the cellar window, sat down and rapped on the door with a piece of wood. 'Malone? You in there?'

'Where else would I be, knobhead. You got some water and maybe some grub? I'm starving.'

'All in good time. You from round here?'

'Not half a mile. Tokky.'

'Really? A proper scouser then. One who can gob in the Mersey from where he was born, like me.'

'You're not a proper scouser. You're a toff and an ex member of the filth fraternity.'

'Okay, Okay, I was going to include you in the scoff order, but if you're going to be like that …'

Silence for a couple of minutes.

'Sorry,' came the voice from inside, quieter now. 'I used to come down this road with me mates to get to the river.'

'Looking for cars to rob or houses to break into?'

'Nah, that came later. I saw big Jimmy Scoular in the local supermarket with his wife. Loaded up his trolley and didn't pay. People were too scared of him to object. I thought, I'm having some of that.'

'Big Jimmy got his bowels blown out with a sawn-off shotgun.'

'I know, but he had a good time while it lasted. I wasn't born with a silver spoon in my gob like some.'

Jack ignored the jibe. 'I was just looking at some old papers,' he said. 'Back from 1998. This girl Sally was supposed to have jumped in the river.'

'I was only eight when she died.' Malone's voice became so quiet that Jack could hardly make out what he was saying. 'There were suspicions that it wasn't suicide,' Malone continued, 'but no one wanted to be a grass.' He laughed, bitterness in his voice. 'Honour among thieves, even when you're eight and not long out of nappies. So what are you saying?'

'I'm saying that Puller had your sister murdered because she knew something vital concerning his aims of going legit. Something that would've put the kybosh on it. And the police helped to cover it up. I'm guessing that Detective Sergeant Tyrer knows something about that. Eddie; we're on the same side.'

CHAPTER THIRTY TWO

Dokka was worried. Alan wasn't answering his phone. Which wasn't like Alan. He was usually quick to answer and relied on Dokka for emotional support, which had been a key part of the conditioning. He knew only one way to resolve this, but Dokka was reluctant to do it. He'd have to track Alan down, wherever he was, and that brought risk. The trouble was, the goods had been delivered, and he'd received the activation message. A decision was needed but, in the meantime, he continued working on his dissertation in the pub.

> *This feeling of paranoia and unease is taken to its extreme in* The Manchurian Candidate. *This film is one of John Frankenheimer's not Pakula's, but it is of its time, released around about the time of the Cuban Missile Crisis and just before the Kennedy Assassination ...*

Dokka made a note to check the dates.

The Manchurian Candidate is one of the most shocking political thrillers of all time. A brainwashed soldier returns home from the Korean war as a hero. His surviving colleagues have unsettling dreams of him shooting two of them in cold blood at the instigation of Russian and Chinese minders. What is real? Who can you trust? In Roman Polanski's Chinatown, *another film from the early seventies, the bad guy is an oligarch who aims to control Los Angeles' water supply. His subjugation of the public good to private greed is reflected in the other theme of the film: incest carried out to wicked extremes. The film was made not long after the Manson killings in which Polanski's pregnant wife, Sharon Tate, was murdered. The director had to be cajoled to come back to Los Angeles and make the film ...*

Dokka made another note to check out the name of the oligarch in *Chinatown*. In the film it was Noah Cross, but in Robert Towne's screenplay it was Julian Cross. JC—it made sense, but then so did Noah.

The dissertation was going well. Soon he could head towards a conclusion.

He tried ringing Alan again, but got no response, so he put the mobile back in the rucksack

on the chair next to him and took a sip of his pint—
not bad, but not as good as the one in the West
Derby pub. This one was deserted and cool,
compared to the heat outside, and just one old feller
sat at the bar—not the one that had aroused his
suspicions in the other place. Strange how these pubs
always had an old feller sitting at the bar at midday
with a pint of lager—it was always lager; why? What
kind of a life was that? Did they have homes to go
to? Did they drink at the same rate all day? They must
be alkies.

Dokka finished his pint, stood up and nearly
fell over when a sharp spasm of cramp cut through
his right leg. He just managed to stay upright and
threw the rucksack over his shoulder. Start with
Alan's flat.

When he drove into the road, he could already
hear the ruckus—screams and shouts coming from
the rear of the flats. Dokka ignored the fuss, parked
up and went in. No answer to the doorbell. He
walked round to the back, in the direction of the
screaming and shouting. What kind of a
neighbourhood was this where you could have such
a fuss at this time of the day? A contested eviction?
A captured burglar? A wooden fence was on fire,
sending a cloud of black smoke into the air. A crowd
of people stood by it, shouting and pointing up at a
window.

'What's going on, mate?' he asked of a young
man in a tracksuit and trainers.

'It's a loony from those flats! We were having a quiet barbecue and he threw a petrol bomb at us. Can you imagine it, lar! A petrol bomb!'

Dokka had a sinking feeling. He walked quickly back to the front entrance and up to the flat.

A bearded man in a suit was banging hard on Alan's door. He turned to Dokka. 'Do you know Mr White?' he said. 'I'm the block supervisor. He's gone and thrown a petrol bomb at those people round the back.'

'I'm a friend of his. Look, you go and placate those people, and I'll try and get him to talk and calm him down.'

'Okay, but the police are on their way.'

Once the supervisor had gone, Dokka got down on one knee and shouted through the keyhole. 'Alan, it's your friend Dokka. Come on, open the door.'

Silence.

'We're under attack,' came a quiet voice from inside.

Dokka thought hard. When he spoke, he did his best to sound reasonable. 'That's right, Alan. We've got to move back to a better position. We're too exposed here.'

After a long silence, the latch turned and the door opened to reveal Alan's frightened face. Dokka sat Alan down on the sofa and fetched him a glass of water.

A knock sounded at the door. Dokka got up and opened it, but only a fraction in case it was the idiots who'd had the bonfire party at the wrong time of the year. A middle-aged man with white hair and a beard stood there. Dokka opened the door wider.

'Sorry,' the man said. 'I've come to help Alan. You are …?'

'A friend of his. And you are?'

'Geoffrey Russell, his social worker. What's been going on? I was called out by the caretaker. You know Alan's a recovering soldier with post-traumatic stress syndrome. He's not to be stressed in any way.' He pulled Dokka out into the corridor and out of sight of Alan, then leaned over and whispered in Dokka's ear. 'He can go suicidal if he's pushed too far.'

'Tell that to the idiots letting off fireworks down there when it's nowhere near bonfire night.'

'Fireworks? Loud noises are the worst possible thing for Alan. What's all this about a petrol bomb?

'Petrol bomb?' News to me.'

They remained close and kept their voices down so Alan couldn't overhear.

'Look,' Dokka whispered. 'I'm a friend of his. I'll look after him.'

Russell looked undecided for a moment. 'Okay,' he said, 'but let's keep things quiet and make sure that he takes his medication. I'll try and pacify those people downstairs.'

Dokka stepped back inside and locked the door. Alan had fallen asleep on the sofa. Dokka sat down opposite him.

If Alan could be quietened down and got back to normal, then they could still follow the original plan. But it would have to be soon. Once Alan was inside the site with Hargreaves's van parked up, Hargreaves out of the way and things quiet, Dokka would ring Alan on his mobile with the code word. Alan would get the tub from the van, drag it inside and tip it into the hatch.

Alan opened his eyes and licked his lips. 'Water,' he said.

CHAPTER THIRTY THREE

Luckily no thump-thump of heavy metal came from the flat next door to the office, but the air conditioning was broken, and it felt unpleasantly hot in the meeting room. Jack opened a window, but this let in a strong smell of cooking chips. He quickly closed it again and made yet another mental note to check out a more salubrious office, though Eddie Malone was probably familiar with a décor of grey carpet, magnolia-painted walls and a veneer table with the edges peeling away, much like your standard police-interview room.

Malone's resemblance to a ferret mesmerised Jack. A dangerous ferret but a ferret none the less, he had a small head, no chin, pointy nose and little beady eyes. He'd be right at home with Freddie the Ferret and his mob.

'So what can you tell us about Mr Puller and his criminal activities, Mr Malone?' Mel asked.

Jack sensed that she wasn't totally convinced by Malone's change of heart. He'd intended that Mel's presence would make him lower his guard, but it seemed to have the opposite effect.

Jack opened his mouth, aiming to ease him into it, but Malone answered without hesitation. 'What do you want to know?' he said. 'Standard organised crime set up. People like me earn the cash, and it's laundered by Johnny Puller via his estates business. Except all the top men on my side are laid up in jail, and Mr Puller is using me and Gobby to further his activities. Like getting rid of headache owners who won't accept a generous offer for their properties—'

'And attempting to murder people who stick their noses in, like Mr Gordon here?' Mel said.

Malone laughed. 'If you stick your nose where it's not wanted, you're liable to get it bitten off. No offence, mate. That was business. Nothing personal.'

'None taken,' Jack said. 'But what about sending Gobby McShrekFace to kidnap my associate, Mrs Gibson, here?'

Malone shrugged. 'He wouldn't have hurt her, just frightened her. Puller's orders.'

'So how does Tyrer fit into this?' Jack asked.

'He's the tame copper. Puller deals with him. Don't worry, if he was involved in my sister's death, then I'll take care of him.'

'Trouble is, he's a copper,' Jack said. 'A key witness, but a copper. Don't go trying to get revenge on him. We need to concentrate on Puller. He's the key to all this, but he'll have to be handled carefully.'

*

When Malone had gone, Jack made coffee and Mel and him had a natter.

'So what do we do now?' Mel asked. 'They were obviously keeping an eye on us—or maybe Oliver Gladwyn or Johnny Puller smelled a rat when we met them.'

'However they did it,' Jack said, 'we obviously can't work inside now.' He thought for a while. 'Puller's the key to Helen's disappearance and the murder of Sally Parker, but you couldn't bring him to justice without involving Tyrer, who will surely bring the weight of the police force down on anyone who tries.'

'And what about Oliver Gladwyn?' Mel said. 'Puller's hold over him probably stems from involvement in various crimes over the years. Like the murder of the informant in Australia. There's no point in chasing that. He went missing in a shark-infested sea, and there's no chance of getting evidence after all this time and under the noses of a foreign police force.' She thought for a moment. 'How do we move forward on this, Jack?'

Jack frowned. 'Hey!' He banged the table with his fist. 'There is one thing. There's a gardener who works for the Gladwyns who fits the description of

214

the family's chauffeur at the time of Helen's disappearance. He's a relative of Freddie's. He's probably involved in the attacks. He was a witness to the party from which Helen disappeared.'

'How do you know that?'

Jack sighed and said nothing for a while. 'After the torching of the Gladwyn's car,' he said eventually, 'I stupidly took Freddie in. He told me all about it.'

'And then what?'

'When I woke up the next morning, he'd gone.'

'You mean you had the villain we are contracted to find and you let him go?'

Jack avoided her gaze. 'Okay, I admit it,' he murmured. 'I fucked up.'

Long silence.

'So the next steps are obvious,' Mel said. 'Check the possible scene of the crime at the lodge and then question this gardener.'

'Right, see what comes out of that, and then deal with Mr Puller and his cop sidekick. Let's get some sleep and get an early start.'

CHAPTER THIRTY FOUR

'So this is where the fateful party was held,' Mel said. 'Nice property; is it listed?'

'Yeah, with the house. Built in the 1830s as an entrance lodge.'

Mel walked around the property with Jack following. 'So where is this Hargreaves now?' she said.

Jack shrugged. 'It's too early in the morning for him to come to this job.'

She walked round the edge of the lodge and stopped before the bulging back wall. That doesn't look too good.'

'Total rebuild.' He laughed. 'I think the builder's taking me for a ride.' He paused. 'Are you thinking what I'm thinking?'

'What? That there's a body behind there?' That's a bit too obvious.'

'Maybe.' He thought. 'He reckons it'll cost twenty thousand.'

'Twenty thousand? Brick not sandstone? He's taking the mickey. I'd have said ten. Max. Who is this builder, anyway?'

'Brian Hargreaves. He's a sole trader.'

'I'll run a check on him. But first we need to question this gardener.'

When they got back to the car, Mel stopped him turning on the engine. 'I've got something to show you.' She reached down, pulled out a laptop, opened it and handed it to him.

'What's all this about, Jack?'

Jack stared at the screen for a good two minutes, then laughed. 'What can I say, Mel. It's all exaggerated. And all these sisters rooting for the little girl hard done by? Okay, there's an element of truth. I'm not a saint.'

'But they're saying that you abandoned your wife and child and that you're avoiding paying what you should.'

He banged his fist on the dashboard, surprising himself. 'You don't know the full story, Mel. The relationship broke down. She used to lie back and think of Germaine Greer. And she wouldn't see reason. Everything was my fault. Ridiculous.'

*

Mel sipped her coffee and worked on her laptop in the passenger seat. Jack drove as carefully as he could, and that wasn't so hard when you were stuck in a line of cars in the outside lane of the A55. His back ached and his eyelids felt heavy. Ahead, heavy black rain clouds gathered over the hills. It was definitely getting cooler. The Cult's *Rain* came to an end and he put on *Everything But The Girl*.

Mel looked up. 'That's better,' she said and went back to her laptop.

'I hope you're not doing further checks on me,' he said.

She sighed. 'Give it a rest, lad. I can see that these women are probably exaggerating, but you don't come out of it smelling of roses. Okay, I'll admit that I'm probably subconsciously on their side because of my own marriage problems. Let's leave it there for now. We've got work to do.' She thought for a moment. 'Now we've been rumbled by Oliver and Johnny, there's no way we can work inside. They pushed you in the river and tried to kidnap me. Nice.' She went back to tapping the keys.

He sighed. 'I don't know how they did it, Mel.'

'Well, however they did it, it's put the kybosh on that line of investigation. Let's hope this lead is more fruitful. And your friend, Mr Brian Hargreaves, is beginning to look like a bit of a scally.'

'Surprise, surprise.'

'I checked his tax and national insurance records,' she continued. 'He's employed as an instructor by a training scheme. They do building work for public bodies like councils, water authorities and the like, training ex-servicemen in building trades so they can get a job in civvy street. Very worthwhile, of course. Except he's doing a foreigner for you. I bet it's not the only one. I've investigated this sort of caper before. They have a nice cushy job and do these foreigners on the side, often using the legit firm's materials.' She looked across at him. 'You can shrug your shoulders, lad, but you and me pay for this this with our taxes. And he's trying to defraud you out of ten grand.'

'Okay,' he said. 'I was a bit of a fool. I'll sort it out when I get back. Let's concentrate on this bad boy of a gardener.'

They'd carefully examined the ordnance survey map before setting off, and both were kitted out for surveillance in outdoor/bird-watcher gear: hiking boots, waterproofs, each with a small rucksack and high-powered binoculars. They parked in a layby on the minor road which ran along the top of the Gladwyn property. Jack had estimated that the road was far enough above the property boundary that you'd get good views of the house itself. As it turned out, they got glimpses of the roof and chimneys of the main house, but that was it. A public footpath led up through open moorland, and they followed this. They came to a small rock outcrop and paused to catch their breath. Jack checked the view through his binoculars.

'This is better!' he exclaimed. 'I can see the area in front of the house. There he is!'

Eric Owen parked a wheelbarrow by a shed, then walked over to a white van.

'Looks like he's packing in for the night.' Jack watched the van move off. He checked his watch. 'Early dart, looks like.' He lost sight of the van, then spotted it again, closer this time.

'It's on this road. Quick! If we leg it, we can get back to the car before he gets there!'

*

Llanwrst was quiet. Rain lashed the streets. The weather had broken at last! Owen went into the co-op. Jack stopped on the half-full car park and waited, watching the rain arrowing horizontally across the street.

Owen left with a six-pack, which he stowed in the van, then he set off again on foot. Mel followed him, but he soon returned with a parcel of what looked like chips. Then he drove for a hundred yards and pulled off onto a hard standing in front of a block of three-storey walk-up flats—the sort of housing built by hard-up city councils in the fifties and sixties.

They parked, watched Owen go up the stairs and got a glimpse of him on the open stairwell going into his flat.

Mel pulled a small rucksack from the back seat. 'Gobby's kidnap kit.' She handed Jack a black balaclava and showed him something small and heavy. 'It's a cosh,' she said. 'From the old days. Fits nice in a pocket. A baseball bat is a bit too obvious.'

They got out and walked up the stairs to the front door to Owen's flat, then pulled their balaclavas over their heads.

Mel looked Jack up and down. 'I don't know about this chauffeur or gardener or whatever he is, but by God you frighten me.'

Owen answered the door and dropped the chip that was on its way to his mouth.

'Just a few questions, Mr Owen,' Jack said through the material of the balaclava.

They frogmarched him into the living room and thrust him into a chair.

Jack looked around. What a tip. Newspapers, magazines everywhere. Half-empty mugs of tea sat on the coffee table, one with a clump of mould floating in it. A magazine with a lady baring an ample bosom on the front page peeked out from under a copy of the *TV Times*. Odd socks lay strewn across the floor, even a pair of dirty-looking underpants. And an acrid, animal smell pervaded everywhere. What a sad man.

There was no point in pretending to be the police, but it was best to act all nice and polite, like police officers, and leave Owen with the feeling that he'd gotten away with something, so he wouldn't complain to anyone.

When Jack mentioned the Gladwyns, Owen's mood changed. 'I had nothing to do with that. It must have been someone who has it in for them.' But when Jack brought up the party in Liverpool, Owen's face went white. 'I don't know anything about that,' he muttered, his voice low.

Mel stood up and pulled something from her pocket. The cosh! She struck Owen across a knee with a loud crack that resounded around the small apartment. Owen screamed, hunched forward, gripped the knee, then straightened up with the pain, his mouth open and his eyes screwed shut. Mel whacked him across the other knee, this time with more of a thump, and Owen collapsed onto the floor. She went into the kitchen and came back with a cup of water. With a sudden movement, she threw it in Owen's face. He cringed back. Mel leant over and gave each knee a hard rap with the cosh. One-two. Owen screamed. Mel giggled. She was enjoying this just a little too much. Jack wondered if he should try and stop her.

'Okay, okay,' Owen gasped. 'It was a wild party. Booze and drugs—you name it. Everyone was pissed or spaced out. Sarah Gladwyn passed out and had to be helped into bed. People were pairing off. Puller was with Helen; it was obvious that she had the hots for him. All the girls fancied him. Something happened. An argument. Oliver Gladwyn was jealous. He must have fancied Helen himself. He caught them in a bedroom. Helen stormed out, packed a bag and set off to catch a taxi to get the train back to Wales. I followed her to the end of the road. She didn't know I was there. Oliver Gladwyn picked her up in his car.'

*

Mel got straight back on the laptop as soon as they started back to Liverpool. 'Well, lookey here!' she said after a few minutes.

'What's up, sweetheart?' Jack said.

'Don't give me that talk, Mr Jumping Jack Flash.' She laughed. 'Looks like the focus has changed for the anarchists. No mention of barrages at the moment. Now it's fracking. Big demo at Crosby at the weekend.'

'Might be an idea to go on that demo,' Jack said. 'Low profile, just check out what people are saying.' He thought. 'You seemed to enjoy working that guy over,' he said after a few moments.

'I got fed up with being battered around and gaslighted by my darling ex-hubby ...' She giggled and turned to catch Jack's look. 'Gaslighting? It's when someone tells you lies and makes you question your own sanity. The crunch came when he started to try and put ideas in my mind about Harriet. Anyway, I went on a self-defence training course. Learned that you need to use excessive violence, go in hard. But not leave any marks. I hit that moron back there across the knees for a good reason—it's very painful, but so long as you don't break the kneecaps, it leaves no obvious marks apart from reddening and bruising which you might get from falling over.' She paused and flexed a fist, probably for effect.

Jack was impressed.

'You need to make them afraid,' she said.

'What if they come back with a knife or a gun?'

'Don't worry, once they're scared, they don't come back. My hubby was a teeth-gnashing psychopath, and he never came back after I creamed his balls for him.'

Jack laughed. 'Sounds like the sort of thing a psychopath would say.'

'No, just a poor woman defending herself.' A long silence passed. 'I suppose you don't like that side of me?' she said.

He didn't reply.

'Okay, that makes us quits, lover boy.'

They both settled back in their seats, deep in thought.

'You know what?' he said at last. 'We need to look behind that wall at the lodge. There could well be a body in there, well, a skeleton after all this time.'

'I was just thinking that myself.'

CHAPTER THIRTY FIVE

Hargreaves's van was parked outside the lodge, but there was no sign of the man himself.

Jack checked his watch—five thirty. Hargreaves would be having his usual extended tea in the Rose Lane café. 'We'll be Okay for at least an hour,' he said to Mel. 'He always has a good scoff.'

They got out of the car, both still in surveillance gear, including cagoules, which was just as well as it looked like rain. Jack got safety helmets and glasses from the car boot.

'What do you reckon happened to Helen Gladwyn?' Mel said. 'If Owen saw Oliver pick her up, then he's the obvious suspect for the murder.'

'On the face of it, but he might've gone around the corner and doubled back. There might've been someone else in the car. All we have is Owen's word for it on something that happened twenty years ago on a cold, dark night when everyone was pissed or stoned. Let's have a look. We've got to be sure.'

The wall seemed to have bulged even more over the few hours since they'd last been there. Jack poked at a brick in the middle of the wall with a shovel. It moved slightly.

'Stand back,' Mel said. 'And put your glasses and your hat on. We don't want a bump on top of that shiner.' She picked up a shovel and swung it at the wall. It whacked into the bricks with a loud clang, taking several with it. The mortar must have totally rotted away. They cleared a hole, but it was dark inside. 'I'll get a torch; there's one in the car,' Mel said.

While she was gone, Jack started to stack loose bricks to one side, but his foot slipped in the mud, and he had to put a hand against the wall to steady himself. The wall moved—too easily. A loud creak sounded, and the whole lot moved towards him. He pushed back with all his strength to stop it coming down on him. 'Help!' he tried to shout, but it came out as a croak. He cleared his throat. 'Help!' he yelled. No response. 'Help!' he roared as loud as he could.

Mel appeared holding a torch.

'The wall's collapsing,' he hissed. 'Get that batten over there.'

She stared at him.

'The one there, the four by two!'

She hauled over the piece of wood. 'We need to wedge it in somehow,' she said, searching around.

'I can't hold it for much longer!' Jack squawked.

Mel came back with a rusty old sledgehammer and soon had the batten wedged in by Jack's ear.

He stepped round to face the wall. 'Here, give it another thump.' He walked a concrete flag over, wedged it against the piece of wood, piled bricks onto the flag and stepped back. 'That should hold it for now.' He took the torch and leaned inside the hole.

'Be careful,' she said.

'Don't worry. He put his head inside and carefully shone the light around, watching for any movement so he could quickly pull back. 'Nothing. Looks like she really did go into the river. He pulled back and stood up. 'That hole needs to be filled in. That wall could kill someone. We need a bricklayer.'

'That's me,' said Mel. 'I picked it up on the building jobs. Not hard once you've got the gist and the right tools. You're just slower than a time-served tradesman. It only needs a dozen bricks to fill that hole. With that prop it should hold it temporarily. It'll need a total rebuild soon. You can be the bricklayer's labourer.' She looked him up and down. 'Unskilled, of course.'

'Trouble is, we've got no tools or materials— cement and that.'

'Let's check the van.'

Picking the lock was easy-peasy for two experienced private dicks.

Mel climbed into the back of the van and selected a bag of ready-mix, a spade and a bricklayer's trowel. 'Let's do the job right,' she said. 'You get a mix going. There's a water tub at the back, and you'll need to find a bucket.' She pulled out a tub of plasticiser. 'Give me a hand with this. Makes it easier to mix and to lay.' She pulled another similar tub forward into the gap. 'Let's not make it immediately obvious that someone's been robbing his van.'

CHAPTER THIRTY SIX

The protest looked like jolly good fun on the BBC News video. The three of them—Jack, Mel and Roy—had gathered to watch it in the meeting room. Although it was well past normal office hours, Jack had called everyone in to review progress. He would've liked to have been on the protest himself, but both he and Mel might be recognised after their cover had been blown. And Roy wouldn't have fitted in. Or maybe he could've played the ageing hippy role. Too late now.

Several hundred people milled around cheerfully at the gates, most carrying placards reading messages such as 'frack off!' They all wore anoraks or carried brollies against the rain lashing down. One protester had climbed to the top of a drilling rig. The camera homed in to where he'd handcuffed himself to a bar and then to his grinning face.

'Look at this bit.' Mel forwarded the video to where two coppers were arresting a smallish man with a short, neatly cut hairstyle—obviously balding at the front—and beard and glasses. He struggled with the coppers, who thrust him into the back of a white police car. The camera framed his face, clearly showing a scar, then a big police hand pushed his head down and around to get him in the car.

For a moment, no one said anything, so Jack kept quiet as well.

Then Roy said, 'Fucking protestors, a mixture of nimbys and anarchists. What's wrong with producing gas in this country rather than importing it from Russia? It's cleaner than coal.'

'Pollution of the water supply?' Mel said. 'Earthquakes? Big lorries thundering down country roads?'

'Name me an energy source that doesn't have problems,' Roy said. 'Nuclear, hydro-electric, coal, wind; they've all got drawbacks.' He paused, an oracle waiting for an audience to settle. 'Nuclear's obvious—the reactor blows up like Chernobyl or Fukushima. Hydro-electric, you drown river valleys and the dammed water silts up. Coal's dirty. Wind turbines are an eyesore, and sometimes the wind don't blow.'

They all contemplated this.

'That's a bit informed for you, Roy,' Jack said. 'Been to the library, have you?'

'No, clever dick. Wikipedia. Marvellous. Facts at your fingertips.'

'Okay,' Jack said. 'So the anarchists have a new focus.'

'Didn't mention the barrage once,' Mel said.

'Any progress with the water boys, Roy?'

'Water boys?'

'The neds who want to poison the water supply of our fair city.'

'This feller claims to be from Romania yet doesn't know its capital city. He's in his thirties, tall and blond, walks with a limp. He's a student, working on a dissertation or something. I got his name— Dmitri Maskhov, but it's probably false. He meets this other guy in the pub. He's in his forties, short and tubby, shaved head, walks with a stick, first name Alan. Right pair of cripples. The pub's the Sefton Castle in West Derby. The feller he meets is on some kind of building-work training scheme. I heard him mention the reservoir.'

Mel and Jack looked at each other.

'Hargreaves does jobs for the water authority,' Mel said.

'I've heard of synchronicity,' Jack said, 'but that's ridiculous.' He turned to Roy. 'Great work, Roy. Now email all this information to Stuart Madison at the NCA. He'll get things organised with the cops.'

The phone rang.

'Got any answers?' Sarah Gladwyn asked. Her voice sounded distant.

'Kind of.'

'What do you mean, kind of? Oliver's due to make a big announcement about the barrage any minute now.'

'Okay. I'll meet you in the pub car park next to the conference centre. Top end by the river. Know it? I'll be there in five minutes.'

CHAPTER THIRTY SEVEN

On the way to the conference centre, Jack noticed a big, silver Merc on his tail. More of Puller's thugs? He suddenly turned off onto a side street without indicating, drove down to the end and turned back to the main road. The Merc followed him. A bit too obviously. Not professionals. He got on the blower to Mel, gave her the description and the registration and asked her to come to the conference centre and check it out.

*

Sarah wore the same dark-blue suit that she'd worn on their first meeting—business lady image: partner of the successful entrepreneur for the presentation. Presumably he'd be announcing the go ahead of the barrage. They wouldn't have called an evening meeting otherwise. Jack felt awed by her presence so close to him in the car. God that was a nice but subtle perfume. The rain had eased off, leaving a glistening-green world around the car park. Occasional drops spattered the roof of the car.

Something stirred in his loins. Should he make a pass?

'Have you got a tissue,' she said, killing the moment. 'I think I'm coming down with a cold.'

'In the glovebox,' Jack said before he realised his mistake.

She saw the revolver and pulled it out with both hands, obviously finding it heavy. 'What's this? Standard issue for private dicks in Liverpool?'

He laughed. 'It's my dad's. From the army. I'd have a nice modern automatic if I needed one. He's terrified of burglars. I took it off his hands.'

She put it back carefully, found a tissue and blew her nose. 'Okay,' she said. 'What do you have to tell me? I need to get to the conference centre for Oliver's presentation.'

He took a deep breath. 'Eric Owen gave us some information—'

'Eric? He's been with the family for years. He's a loyal member of staff.'

'He was at the party where your sister disappeared. Taking everything in. She was supposed to catch a taxi, but Eric saw Oliver pick her up in his car.'

A long silence ensued while she took this in, after which she sat up, looked towards the back of the car, then turned her head so that her face was a foot from his. Her eyes were no longer green and sparkling but empty and black like those of a shark he'd once seen on the TV. 'What was that?' she said. 'There's someone behind the car!'

Jack jumped out and edged around the car. He caught a glimpse of Sarah running across the car park, leaving the driver's door and the glove box open. The pistol was gone.

He raced after her.

The conference centre was packed—the main hall all yellow wood and glass with the view out over a grey, featureless Mersey.

Oliver Gladwyn was coming to the end of his speech. He turned off the overhead just as Jack was trying to read it. The lights came on, showing Gladwyn at a lectern and a load of dignitaries ranged on chairs on the stage behind him.

'So, ladies and gentlemen, to recap. We've taken on board the eel issue …' Titters of laughter came from around the hall. 'We've redesigned the fish ladder so that our silvery, slippery friends can get up and down it to their heart's content.'

Jack caught a movement out of the corner of his eye. Sarah Gladwyn strode purposefully down the aisle until she stood a few feet from Oliver who stepped back.

She raised the revolver, held in both hands.

Click. The safety was on.

She fumbled with the gun for a moment—
Jack wondered if some gallant gentleman of the old
school might help her out.

Oliver stepped back. 'Why, Sarah?'

She found the catch.

The report reverberated around the hall,
leaving a cloud of smoke and dust.

The panicking crowd swept Jack along. Once
out the door, the crowd fanned out, and Jack turned
to go back in. A hand grabbed his shoulder and
turned him round to see Tyrer's grinning face.

'Steady as you go, matey! Mr Puller would like
a word with you.' Before he knew it, Jack was cuffed
with his hands behind him, and he was being
marched over the tarmac. They passed a police car—
empty apart from Eddie Malone sitting in the back.
He looked apologetic.

'Plea bargain,' he mouthed at Jack.

CHAPTER THIRTY EIGHT

'Let's be having you, Gordon,' Tyrer sneered. He dragged Jack from the unmarked cop car, pushed him face down on the bonnet and removed the cuffs—now that would give the game away when the body is fished out of the river, Jack thought—then he pulled one of Jack's arms behind his back. Johnny Puller appeared from nowhere and leaned over.

'Flash Gordon,' he whispered in Jack's ear. 'Or is that Jumping Jack Flash? You won't be doing much flashing or jumping where you're going.'

'It's your favourite method, isn't it?' Jack said, his face inches from Puller's. 'You and Oliver Gladwyn, making drowning look like suicide. Helen Gladwyn, Sally Parker and that poor feller you fed as bait for the sharks in Australia. What was his name, Johnny?'

Puller grinned. 'Wouldn't you like to know?' he said brightly. 'Well, why not make it four. And, actually, that hippy Gladwyn didn't have the balls to do it,' he whispered. 'I was in the car with him when we picked the tart up. She wouldn't go along with the nice threesome we had in mind. I lost my temper and strangled her in the back of the car. Oliver panicked and ran off. I had to tidy things up.' He laughed. 'Shame there's no sharks here. We'll have to make do with eels. They take a bit longer but in the end the job gets done.'

Tyrer frogmarched Jack to the edge of the walkway with his hand twisted behind his back and his feet slipping on the wet tarmac. The brown water seethed with white flecks of foam. Jack looked upstream. An ominous hump of water, maybe two metres high, was approaching—the Mersey Bore—fed by the recent torrential rain in the hills.

Jack caught a glimpse of Puller following, holding the pistol. Tyrer twisted Jack's head around just in time for Jack to see a figure rush up. A large, meaty, red face thrust into Jack's. What did they call them? Gammons?

'You bastard, Gordon! I got the papers this morning. I'm going to be fleeced for every penny I've got. All on account of your nasty work!'

Morgan leaned back and swung a punch at Jack. The punch was a beauty, or it would've been if Jack hadn't ducked, suddenly terrified of the prospect of a blow on his damaged face. The shot thumped into the copper's jaw. Jack fell to one side and lay watching as Morgan grabbed Tyrer and pushed him towards the river. Tyrer kept hold of Jack's coat pulling him with them. They collided with Puller and the three of them went into the river.

Not again! Jack's only feeling was one of irritation at going in the drink one more time—but with the difference that maybe this time he'd be washed clean of his sins. As they hit the water, the hand holding Jack's coat loosened its grip. He twisted free and tried to hold his breath. He was learning. He surfaced and gasped for air, finding himself on the crest of the bore, moving fast. No one else to be seen.

Something landed on his head—a life buoy. He grabbed it and held on against the force of the bore, then it jerked tight and he was being reeled in like a fish. As he neared the side, he could see Mel's face, grinning down at him.

'Ah, Flash Gordon,' she said. 'You're lucky I keep an eye on what you're up to. And you're not coming out of there until you promise to do right by all those ladies you've left in the lurch.'

Jack opened his mouth, but it filled with water. 'Okay! Okay!' he spluttered.

He took her hand, scrambled over the edge of the stone parapet and lay gasping for air, water running from his sodden clothes.

'Have you drunk much of that water?' she said. 'I know they've cleaned up the river but that looks foul.'

He shook his head, snorting up a great mouthful of snot.

'Well,' she said. 'I suppose I'll have to give you mouth to mouth resuscitation, then.' She got down onto her knees but couldn't get into position. She almost toppled over and had to put a hand on his groin. 'I notice that you're glad to see me,' she said, her voice as dry as a fistful of desert sand after a six-year drought.

CHAPTER THIRTY NINE

'Well, your nose has healed up nicely.' Stuart Madison leaned forward and sipped his coffee. He pulled a face. 'Coffee's shite as usual. But what's with the black eye?' He leaned back in his seat outside the café and surveyed the Liverpool suburban street with its pavements glistening from overnight rain. The sky was heavy and overcast. It looked like it might rain again soon.

Stuart wore a light-blue tie, dark-blue suit and white shirt, and he'd swapped his yellow brogues for a pair of carefully polished, black leather shoes—not even pointy ones. Quite the well turned out little National Crime Agency operative now. Promotion on the cards?

Jack winced. 'Just a domestic disagreement,' he said after some thought. He felt like a new man now that he was getting plenty of sleep. Sleeping like a baby, in fact. As for the black eye, he'd tried claiming that he'd walked into a door, but all he'd got were raised eyebrows and little smiles. So best tell the truth and laugh it off. And it'd been a peach of a punch from Mel. It was a spicy relationship but dangerous.

'And it's an awful view,' Stuart continued. 'Though I must say I prefer it damp and cool like this rather than that awful heat wave we had a couple of weeks back. Can't understand why British people want sun all the time. I like it cool. That's the one thing wrong with going abroad.' He looked like he wanted to take another sip of coffee but thought better of it.

'Well, Jack,' he continued. 'You delivered in time and within budget. We circulated the descriptions and information your lad Roy provided, and we got them. The police felt Dokka the minder's collar at the airport. He tried to run, but it turned out he has two artificial legs. Lost them in the Chechnyan war. We nabbed poor little Alan from where he was hiding in a toilet. Seems like the poor feller was brainwashed after he was captured in Iraq. The shrinks can't entirely reverse brainwashing, but they'll give it a go. We got a link to a private hospital in Pakistan—really a front for the brain-washing operation. The Yanks blew it up with a cruise missile strike—typical American over-reaction. We could've found out much more if we'd captured it intact and interrogated the staff. Anyway, we prevented a major attack on the water supply of a major Western city.'

He sniffed and surveyed the street. 'If you can call Liverpool a major Western city. And the outbreak of severe constipation took some explaining. Even though it wasn't deadly, and everyone recovered after a few days.' He laughed. 'Apparently it wasn't poison, it was plasticiser.'

'Plasticiser?'

'Yeah, the stuff they put in cement mortar. You know. To lay bricks.'

It was Jack's turn to laugh. 'Plasticiser in the water supply wouldn't cause mass constipation, would it? Across a city the size of Liverpool?'

Stuart shrugged. 'I know, but it leaked out that someone had put something in the water supply. Some kind of placebo, homeopathic effect. Mass hysteria.' He laughed. 'Something like that. I don't suppose you know anything about Detective Inspector Tyrer and pillar of the local business community,

Johnny Puller, drowning in the river not far away from the shooting? The Merseyside police are not happy about that. No? Anyway, I think we can take you on a full-time contract. I'll email you through the papers. Don't go broadcasting it around. Let's just keep it to ourselves.'

Jack wondered if it really was all sorted. Sarah was in jail with her trial due shortly. Surely she'd be dealt with leniently. Manslaughter rather than murder. Diminished responsibility or whatever. And the irony was that she'd killed the wrong man, her husband, for Helen's murder. What a mess. It seemed that Freddie and the anarchists had lost interest in the Gladwyns when they heard that Oliver had been shot and Sarah sent to jail. Honour had been served, it seemed.

Jack had followed the barrage issue in the news, and it looked like it was still a goer, with another green entrepreneur about to step in and take it over. Though Wirral Wanderers had reverted to traditional management and catering—bacon butties, cups of Oxo and sweet tea at half time.

'Well, thank you for that, Stuart. Could you cc our new joint chief executive officer, Mel Gibson, with the details?'

'What, the Australian-Scottish freedom fighter from *Braveheart*?' He burst out laughing. 'To go along with Jumping Jack Flash Gordon?'

Jack contemplated this, then said, trying hard but not quite successfully to keep the dryness out of his voice: 'Well I've never heard that one before …'

At that moment it started to rain, sudden heavy drops, each hitting the pavement with a slap. Just like *3.10 to Yuma* at the end.

THANK YOU FOR READING
Pool of Life

If you enjoyed reading this novel, please consider leaving a review on Amazon. It's also available as an e-book.

You can contact me direct to tell me what you thought of *Pool of Life*:

Post on my Facebook page:
www.facebook.com/PeteTrewinAuthor
e-mail me via my website:
http://www.petetrewin.com

My website has information on forthcoming novels and some background to the north of England settings in my books. There is also information on my interests which range from conservation of historic buildings to rock climbing.

Do you want to be notified of new releases?
If so, please sign up to the AIA Publishing email list. You'll find the sign-up button on the right-hand side under the photo at www.aiapublishing.com. Of course, your information will never be shared, and the publisher won't inundate you with emails, just let you know of new releases.

Acknowledgments

Tahlia Newland for editing.
Barbara Scott Emmett for proof reading and formatting.
Ned Hoste of 2H Design for the cover design.
Paula Trewin for beta reading and support.
Ian Grady for beta reading and humour.